Readers love *A Day Makes*
by MARY CALMES

"Once again, Mary
Calmes has written a
book that I couldn't
put down."
　　　—Under the Covers
　　　　　Book Blog

"Few could pull this
off. Mary is one of
them."
　　　—Gay Book Reviews

A DAY
MAKES

"*A Day Makes* is just
fabulous. It is exciting, romantic, sexy, and totally captivating."
　　　　　　　　　　　　　　　　　　　—Joyfully Jay

More praise for
MARY CALMES

Old Loyalty, New Love

"It was refreshing to read a story about a different type of shifter. I loved that Ms. Calmes managed to create a whole new world with new shifters, culture and customs… It was amazing!"

—The Blogger Girls

"*Old Loyalty, New Love* elevates the genre. A well written contemporary—check, a multi-layered paranormal—check, and lastly, a poignant, sensual love story—check and mate."

—Joyfully Reviewed

Chosen Pride

"Fans of this unique take on shifters will undoubtedly enjoy this story as much as I did. I hope that we get to see more of this world because it's endlessly fascinating to me."

—The Novel Approach

"I ate it up and was begging for more."

—Gay Book Reviews

When the Dust Settles

"Smokin' hot and such a wonderful treat for Mary Calmes's fans!"

—Hearts on Fire Reviews

"With typical Mary Calmes finesse and skilled writing, this book will make you fall in love with Glenn, Stef and Rand, and all the rest of the cowboys on the Red Diamond ranch all over again."

—Diverse Reader

By MARY CALMES

Acrobat
Again
Any Closer
With Cardeno C.: Control
With Poppy Dennison: Creature Feature
Floodgates
Frog
Grand Adventures (Dreamspinner Anthology)
The Guardian
Heart of the Race
Ice Around the Edges
Judgment
Just Desserts
Lay It Down
Mine
Romanus • Chevalier
Romanus & Chevalier (Paperback Only Anthology)
The Servant
Steamroller
Still
Tales of the Curious Cookbook (Multiple Author Anthology)
Three Fates (Multiple Author Anthology)
What Can Be
Where You Lead
Wishing on a Blue Star (Dreamspinner Anthology)
You Never Know

CHANGE OF HEART
Change of Heart • Trusted Bond • Honored Vow
Crucible of Fate • Forging the Future

Published by DREAMSPINNER PRESS
www.dreamspinnerpress.com

By MARY CALMES (CONT.)

L'ANGE
Old Loyalty, New Love • Fighting Instinct • Chosen Pride

MANGROVE STORIES
Blue Days • Quiet Nights • Sultry Sunset
Easy Evenings • Sleeping 'til Sunrise
Mangrove Stories (Print Only Anthology)

MARSHALS
All Kinds of Tied Down • Fit to Be Tied • Tied Up in Knots

A MATTER OF TIME
A Matter of Time: Vol. 1 • A Matter of Time: Vol. 2
Bulletproof• But For You
Parting Shot • Piece of Cake

TIMING
Timing • After the Sunset • When the Dust Settles
Perfect Timing (Print Only Anthology)

THE VAULT
A Day Makes • Late in the Day

THE WARDER SERIES
His Hearth • Tooth & Nail • Heart in Hand
Sinnerman • Nexus • Cherish Your Name
Warders Volume One • Warders Volume Two

Published by DREAMSPINNER PRESS
www.dreamspinnerpress.com

LATE
IN THE
DAY

Mary Calmes

DREAMSPINNER
PRESS

Published by

DREAMSPINNER PRESS

5032 Capital Circle SW, Suite 2, PMB# 279, Tallahassee, FL 32305-7886 USA
www.dreamspinnerpress.com

Late in the Day
© 2017 Mary Calmes.

Cover Art
© 2017 Reese Dante.
http://www.reesedante.com
Cover content is for illustrative purposes only and any person depicted on the cover is a model.

ISBN: 978-1-64080-428-9
Digital ISBN: 978-1-63533-980-2
Library of Congress Control Number: 2017914125
Published October 2017
v. 1.0

Printed in the United States of America

This paper meets the requirements of
ANSI/NISO Z39.48-1992 (Permanence of Paper).

For Lynn, who is on my journey with me, Lisa,
who makes everything better, and Susan,
who answers odd questions about her home.

CHAPTER ONE

SOMETIMES IN life, being a person's protector translated into trivial situations like making sure they called when they got home safely after leaving your place for the night. At other times caretaking took on a more life-or-death connotation. Me looking after Trevan Bean was the latter, which was why I came along to what appeared, on the surface, like a normal everyday meeting with his fairly new boss, Marc Eastman.

"You know," Trevan teased—he'd learned to do that over the course of our acquaintance—"having you come with me is like bringing a gun to a knife fight."

"You're saying I'm overkill?"

"Yeah," Trevan said, grinning wolfishly. "That's what I'm saying."

Once upon a time, he'd been terrified of me. That had stopped years ago, which said more about me and how scary I *wasn't* anymore than anything else.

It made sense. I was tired. Though I didn't like to admit it, after twenty-plus years of killing for my country under the umbrella of the military, and then for profit as a private contractor, I was more than ready to quit. The chances of that happening, of everyone letting me quietly walk away, had been, originally, slim to none. As a rule, contract killers didn't retire; someone retired *them*. The fact that I would be spared that was still very new, a blessing that had blindsided me. It wasn't, however, only my good fortune. The man we were there to see was also reaping the rewards of my newfound lease on life. Had I still been thinking I had no future, I would have been far less patient with him.

When we reached the penthouse on the slowest elevator in existence and I exited, I counted five men in the room—not including Marc Eastman and his second-in-command, David Seta, who were sitting out on the balcony, Eastman on his phone. Conspicuously missing was Dean Fortney, Eastman's muscle, the guy in charge of security. It looked ominous.

One of the men waved Trevan and me outside onto the balcony that looked out toward Ren Cen. It meant all those men between us and the door, but I was still pleased to have a great view of all the other buildings. It meant Ceaton Mercer, my number two, my guardian at meetings like this one, would have no trouble making sure Trevan and I remained healthy. Eastman had no clue whom he was truly dealing with. Sadly, that ignorance would end with this meeting.

Gesturing for Trevan to go ahead of me as I trailed behind him, I noted the sharp contrast between the white rugs, furniture, and walls in Eastman's home and the black overcoats Trevan and I wore. I wasn't crazy about the target we presented, but between myself and Ceaton in the next building, I was pretty confident that even if Eastman's men drew down on us that we would be all right. The odds were in our favor.

Once outside, we took seats across from Trevan's boss. It was fortunate we were still wearing our overcoats because it was cold outside, somewhere in the twenties. Yesterday it had been warmer, up in the fifties, but the temperature plummeted overnight and hadn't come back up.

"Why are we out here," I groused under my breath, irritated, hating the cold almost as much as the cloying humidity of summer.

"I prefer it actually," Trevan answered my rhetorical question. "I mean, it feels like a fishbowl in there. At least out here we can breathe."

"It's March," I muttered, still grouchy, having not had enough coffee yet. "Jesus."

Trevan chuckled beside me. "It's Detroit."

I grunted.

"I think you hate the cold more than anyone I know."

It made me foul; there was no way around that. I should have planned to move to Florida instead of Boston because that was like going from the frying pan into the fire, but I had already made the plans to leave Detroit very soon.

"Seriously," Trevan teased me. "Maybe the city we want is Honolulu."

"Shut up," I ordered.

"Trevan," Eastman greeted warmly after ending his call, standing from behind a heavy cut-glass table with beveled edges, hand held out for my friend to take.

Trevan stayed seated and kept his arms crossed, no longer needing to make nice with the guy who'd killed his old boss, his first boss, the man he would have walked through fire for, trusting me when I said his family was safe and his husband, Landry Carter, already in Boston, was just as secure.

"No?" Eastman said snidely, spurring laughter and snickering around us. "You don't even want to touch me anymore?"

"I never wanted to," Trevan assured him, "but now I don't have to because I'm leaving the city after this."

"You don't go anywhere without my say so, little boy."

Trevan scoffed. "Watch me."

Eastman's gaze darted to me, and I watched guys moving to stand behind me out of the corner of my eye.

"You should have them be still," I suggested. "Don't want everyone ending up like Fortney."

He jolted—it wasn't subtle—and Seta, beside him, went ashen. "Where's Fortney?" Eastman asked shakily.

"Call and find out."

Everyone froze as Eastman turned to his second-in-command, who pulled his phone from the breast pocket of his suit jacket.

"I need to check something," I said, opening my hand and extending it out to my side. The small red dot that hit it caused murmurs on the balcony and in the room next to us, gasps, and Seta whimpered as he spoke while Eastman quickly crossed his arms.

"What is this?" he asked sharply, no power in his voice, more a rasp.

"This is me wanting you to understand that everyone here is alive right now because I'm allowing it. Move your guys back where I can see them or I'll have my colleague start shooting."

Everyone complied quickly and moved to the opposite side of the balcony or room behind Eastman.

Seta placed his phone facedown on the table.

"Well?" Eastman prodded anxiously, brows furrowed, lips pursed, just the picture of unease. What's going on?"

"Fortney's dead," Seta reported.

Eastman had a pretty good poker face, but when he glanced at me as well, he caught his breath. The quick swallow was not something I missed either.

"Just dead?" I asked Seta, wanting my intent to be clear.

He cleared his throat. "No. You left him in pieces."

"Not me," I clarified, smiling smugly, laying it on. "My guy."

"Why would he do that?"

I shrugged. "I asked him to send a message."

"And what was that?"

I turned to Trevan.

"What?" Trevan repeated.

"Fortney killed Pike," I told him flatly.

"He was the one?"

I nodded.

"Thank you for finding out."

I returned my attention to Eastman and Seta. "Trevan asked me to find the man who killed Pike and then to make sure that he got the same—and more—that his mentor did."

Eastman took a breath through his nose.

"I didn't want you to miss retribution when you saw it," I stated flatly.

His hands closed tightly over the ends of the armrests on his chair. "You realize that I have twenty men here in the penthouse with us and even more just one floor below."

"The man covering my back is a surgeon with a rifle in his hand, and at the moment he has the most expensive scope in the world mounted on it. I know that because I bought it for him a little over a month ago as a housewarming present."

He shivered. It was subtle—I only saw it because I was watching so closely.

"Plants are so cliché, don't you think?"

"I'm going to kill you," Eastman promised.

"You're not." I was implacable. "Because if I do anything but sit here and smile, my guy will send an RPG into the floor below after he kills every last person left alive here."

"You think he can shoot that fast?"

"He doesn't have to do anything fast. He'll just kill whoever's left once I'm done."

Eastman paled.

"I have a gun too. I'm not just going to sit here and let you draw down on me or Trevan. You're insane if you think that could ever happen."

"You're so confident in your associate?"

"I didn't say associate. I said he was *my guy*, and that makes all the difference here with what lengths he's prepared to go to."

Ceaton Mercer was, in fact, my knight, the guy who kept me safe. It was a brand-new arrangement. A contract killer would not normally have backup, but I'd taken a new job, a permanent one, thus the push to get Trevan out of the Motor City.

Trevan wasn't sure. He'd lived his whole life in Detroit, and the idea of leaving the city, his city, was scary. But I was sure it was the right thing to do, and because he wanted the man he loved safe, as well as his family, he was doing as I directed and going forward with plans to uproot his life and move to Boston so he could remain under my protection.

"Why there?" he asked that morning in the car as we drove toward downtown.

"Because I found this island I like that's quiet," I replied mildly, "but it's also close to the city, so you can find a place to do your restaurant thing and Landry can relocate his jewelry business."

Trevan nodded like that made sense. And I knew it did. Logic and I were very well acquainted. But still, I knew he was hurting. It was hard to leave, harder to start over, and he was angry that he had to. But he was out of choices.

It always went that way when a person began to legitimize a previously illegitimate business. Someone wasn't happy. In the case of my friend, Trevan Bean, he had been trying to get out of the gun trafficking business for the past two years. Slowly, flying under the radar, he'd been liquidating illegal inventory—firearms and explosives—and changing it over into legal inventory at a lesser profit, still with money always coming in. He had some creative accounting going so that no one was any the wiser at the moment, but I'd been certain that a reckoning was coming. When Trevan told me he had a meeting he couldn't get out of, I knew the time had arrived.

I, of course, understood the impetus behind the change. Two years ago, Gabriel Pike, Trevan's mentor, had been killed execution-style when Thiago Fanton came to Detroit and eliminated the Masada crime family's hold in a wave of blood that left no boss standing. Trevan wasn't originally targeted because he wasn't far enough up the food chain. He was only the guy who managed the runners who collected gambling debts as well, but his job changed as soon as Eastman realized what he had. Trevan was smart, and he could do his job in his sleep. He was moved immediately up to logistics, became the guy who tracked what inventory came in and went out, and in that capacity, he became invaluable to not only Eastman, but Eastman's boss, Fanton.

Thiago Fanton, a member of the Gaeta crime family out of New York, wanted all the guns and gambling business in Detroit and he was adding drugs and girls to the mix, something Trevan and the rest of the Masada crew weren't involved in before. There was big money in meth, cocaine, and prostitution, and the new Italian mob now fighting with the guys already there was taking the business in that direction. What had hurt Trevan the most was that initially Gabriel told him he'd be given the choice to leave on his own terms. Gabriel planned his departure. He sent his family ahead to California, but he never joined them. After three days, his wife contacted Trevan, who alerted the police to his disappearance.

A week later, Gabriel's body had been identified and the grisly details recounted to Trevan—because he was the one to file the missing person report. Having to call Gabriel's wife, a woman he knew, shredded him up inside. I sat beside him in his office, my hands on his shoulders as he broke down sobbing afterward.

"They killed him because he didn't want to become a pimp and a drug dealer," he cried.

"I know, kid," I tried to soothe him.

He heaved out a breath. "I'm going to fix this."

I didn't even want to guess what that meant. It wasn't my area. My only job was to protect him from anyone who wanted to hurt him and make them pay if they tried. It was one of many hats I wore.

"I won't lose anyone else."

He lost his father when he was young, and losing Gabriel was almost more than he could bear. "I swear to God, Con," he said sadly, his voice nasally from crying. "I'm gonna get out of this fuckin' business in one piece, but first off, I'm gonna make it legit so no one will ever be able to tie me to anything dirty."

I sat quietly beside him and let him alternate between tears and rage. It was my role.

A week later, as I stood beside him at the steel mill on Zug Island, I asked him if he was sure about his course of action.

"I am."

So I gave the go-ahead, and we watched as molten steel was poured over weapons that Trevan Bean was responsible for selling. Anything from Glocks to Uzis, AK-47s to shotguns and rocket launchers to revolvers were destroyed. Millions of dollars were gone in seconds and as we walked out I was silent.

"You're worried about me, about my choices," he said quietly.

"I am."

He cleared his throat. "I know you didn't sign on for this, so if you can't have my back anymore I—"

"This changes nothing," I muttered, keeping my voice low, comforting. "I've pledged to keep you safe, and I will. I'm just wondering what your plan is."

"Plan for what?" he asked, turning to look at me.

"I get destroying the guns, but what are you putting in their place?"

His smile was wicked. "I do have a thought."

I was really only slightly concerned.

Eighteen months later and people were starting to catch on, so I was taking him out of Detroit before anyone got around to coming after him. Not that he wasn't on everyone's list to get rid of, but to get to him, they had to go through me.

That was easier said than done, but they had begun trying.

It started out so small that I had barely noticed at first.

I had a near miss in a parking garage, and a day later, a drunk almost ran me down as I was crossing a street in Chinatown. A week after that, a guy tried to mug me. So stupid. When he was dead, as I checked the gun he'd pulled on me, I realized the firearm cost more than what I had on me. If I hadn't been so preoccupied with the logistics of moving Trevan, finding the man I wanted to be my backup as I moved into my new position, and looking for a house for myself in the Boston area—I probably would have realized sooner that these were actual attempts on my life. But as it was, when I was tailed for three blocks in the dead of winter and the car came up onto the sidewalk after me—no pretending, no swerving, just without a doubt trying to run me down—well, then they had my attention.

Of course, after that incident, after I left four dead men in an Oldsmobile in an alley… then things escalated.

Five guys were in my condo when I got home from driving Trevan to a meeting, so I went upstairs to my neighbor's place—a very sweet flight attendant who was never home—went out onto her balcony and literally got the drop on them. It was exhausting, killing men with a knife, but a gun would have been too noisy, even with a suppressor, and digging bullets out of bodies was a pain in the ass.

The blood was a whole other annoyance. Luckily I found the vehicle they'd come in—it was parked conspicuously in a guest spot in the resident lot—and loaded the dead men into the Chevy Suburban. I was really quite appreciative of all the space. After the fifth time up and down the stairs, I was beat. Even guys like professional soccer players who did tons of cardio, would have been tired after that.

I left the Suburban under an overpass, ablaze, and then burned everything I'd worn when I got home. The quickest way to get caught was to transfer something from a crime scene to home, so I stripped down at the front door, leaving every stitch outside—it was late, after all—then changed, returned to my welcome mat, gathered everything I'd worn, head to toe, and took it to the basement and charred it to ash in the furnace.

Now, a week later, I was escorting Trevan to an early morning meeting with Eastman, the guy Fanton had put in charge before he returned to New York, satisfied that his new man could hold down the fort in the Motor City. The meeting took Eastman three weeks to set up because Trevan had been ducking his calls and working very hard to hide without looking like he was.

It wasn't easy to make so much inventory disappear, but Trevan had done it, slowly, carefully, methodically, saying no when people made inquiries, sounding sincerely apologetic when he told them that sadly, his inventory had already been sold. That was the same story month after month, that the weapons had all been bought at one time and Trevan didn't have any more to sell. After a year of being told no, people stopped asking, but as far as Eastman and Fanton knew, they were still in the gun business. What they didn't know was the warehouses that used to stockpile AK-47s and RPGs now were full of dog food and lumber, automobile parts and office supplies. They were all rented out, and now, finally, he'd sold all of them, the last sale going yesterday with all the money funneled to New York through an account that was set up when Fanton first hit town. Trevan didn't take a dime. Stealing money wasn't the point. What he'd succeeded in doing was dismantling the business he had helped grow.

But now I couldn't stand around being his guardian angel anymore and so had made provisions for him. It was why Fortney was dead. I needed to get things moving.

"Darius?" Trevan whispered, using my birth name, but under his breath, not wanting the others to hear it. He was already in the habit of using it.

"We're fine," I assured him, returning my attention to Eastman.

He fisted his hands in front of him, breathing through his nose, before he turned back to Trevan. "You are a very fortunate man, Trevan."

"Yessir, I know," he agreed solemnly. "Do you want to talk business now?"

"The only business I want to talk about is *where are all my fucking guns?*" he roared, pushed to the breaking point.

"They're not your fucking guns. They're Mr. Fanton's fucking guns, and they're gone, every last one of them," he replied, pulling an envelope from the breast pocket of his suit jacket and passing it to Seta. "Inside you'll find all the deed transfers and the rest of the paperwork that documents the sale of all the warehouses and the balance of the commercial property here in Detroit."

"What are you talking about?" Eastman barked.

Trevan leaned forward, holding his gaze. "No one ever checks in this business. Gabriel had that motto that you hear all the time: inspect what you expect. But not you guys. Nobody ever came to the warehouses, nobody ever wanted to take a tour with me. All you guys cared about was that the money came in. And yeah, it was less, but not a hundred thousand dollars less."

"I don't understand what…." Eastman turned to Seta, snatching the piece of paper Seta had extracted from the envelope from his hands. "What are you saying?"

"I'm saying that everything is gone."

"I don't understand."

"There are no guns," he explained, "and now there are no warehouses."

He stared at Trevan blankly.

"First, I got rid of the weapons and had us selling anything that was overstocked at rock bottom prices," he continued. "I sold furniture, lumber, farm equipment, power tools—I mean, really, it looked like a Home Depot or a Lowe's—it was nuts."

"You're not making any sense."

Trevan huffed out a breath. "I had to move ten times more garden fertilizer and dog food and cat litter than I did guns, but I kept the money close enough that no one asked me any questions. You only wanted to talk to me after Mr. Fanton heard that no one was buying guns from his guy in Detroit anymore, only in other cities."

Eastman nodded, wiping sweat from his forehead, looking more and more nervous by the second.

"Yeah, that's what I figured," Trevan said with a nod. "So I haven't moved any guns in over a year."

Eastman was even paler than usual and looked unsteady in his chair. Seta's face was screwed up like he was constipated or ready to pass out, the way his eyelids kept fluttering. Both of them were reeling.

"As I said, in that envelope you'll find bills of sale. All the warehouses have been sold off and belong legally not to the people who work there—because I know how you guys work and didn't want them strong-armed—but by large corporations, some not even in this country. So if you did try and talk to the people there, you'd see that in each case, the warehouses are impossible to get back by any other means besides legal and with a large amount of cash changing hands."

Both men were staring at him utterly horrified.

"And I mean a fuckton of it," Trevan added. "Not that I can see Mr. Fanton wanting to spend a lot of money getting back something he used to own."

No one said a word.

"Seems counterintuitive," Trevan continued. "But I guess if Mr. Fanton asks, you can tell him that under your watch, all of his warehouses and the business that went along with it… were shut down in Detroit."

The prolonged silence from the two men wasn't surprising. They'd been completely blindsided, it would take long minutes for them to come up with any sort of intelligent rebuttal.

"Or just don't tell him anything and say you have to pull out of Detroit for other reasons."

I did a slow pan to Trevan, because he could stop talking at any point now. There was no reason to go rubbing what he'd done in their faces. One of them might just stand up and try and shoot him on general principal, and then I'd have to stop them, and then we'd be in the middle of a bloodbath just because he couldn't stop poking the bear.

"What?" Trevan asked after a moment, realizing I was scowling at him.

"Are you done?" It was a question, but I was also prodding him.

"I was just trying to think of what he could say," he said defensively. "You know I always try and consider all the alternatives."

It was true; he did. But now was not the time. I shook my head. "Wrap it up."

Trevan cleared his throat and looked back at Eastman. "I wanted to be out after Gabriel was killed. I told you that a million times."

Still nothing from Eastman or Seta. I was certain that the magnitude of what Trevan had been able to accomplish right under their noses was a hard pill for the men to swallow. But so many people were just like them—watching the money and nothing else.

"I was happy. Everything was going well and I would have stayed and been loyal, and not first legitimized your business and then simply ended it, if you hadn't killed Gabriel," Trevan informed them.

"The fact that you did what you did to him made me want to hurt you in the only way I could."

Shock covered Eastman's face.

"The last of the money coming through will be in the account at the end of this month. After that, there's nothing else," Trevan explained, sucking in a quick breath. "You can, of course, try and rebuild that part of the business here in Detroit, but after all this time of me saying no… I'm not sure who would want to traffic guns with you or trust you to—"

"I get it," Eastman said icily, cutting him off. "You've burned the house down."

"Yes."

"Mr. Fanton will bury you," he dared to threaten the man I'd been watching over for almost three years.

"He won't," Trevan assured him. "He'll be too busy wondering about your incompetence. He'll wonder why you never checked on me, not even once."

"You—"

"It's true," he insisted. "He won't look past you to me. He'll assume you killed me for what I did to you, and he won't even check why you didn't."

Eastman swallowed hard. "Even if that's true, he'll come for you once I'm out of Detroit."

"But I won't be here by the time he figures that out, and even if he comes looking for me in my new city…." Trevan sighed before tipping his head toward me. "You know."

Eastman glanced at me, solid and present beside the man he wanted to not only kill anymore, I was sure, but annihilate.

"So, are you and I done?" Trevan asked.

"Oh yeah, kid, you're done."

I would have rolled my eyes—it was so stupid and over the top—but I just wanted to get out of there without killing anyone. It would be a hassle I didn't care enough about.

Rising from the table, Trevan walked from the patio toward the door, the slow rise and fall of his walk a smooth, seamless glide. He really was a beautiful kid, a blend of his African-American father and Cuban mother with chiseled features and warm brown eyes.

I'd always found him handsome in a distracted way. I'd seen him as someone to watch over, to protect, from the start, and after our association moved from acquaintance to friendship, I saw him as a little brother and nothing more. People misjudged him all the time, thought he looked tough and wary, like a street thug instead of the enterprising businessman he truly was. I had never done that because from the first moment we'd met, I'd seen him use his brain and not his brawn.

He, on the other hand, had seen me first as scary, then beautiful—his word, not mine—and finally, now, sort of a mixture of both.

"It's your eyes," he told me once, sitting beside me in my car, "it's the gold with the green, against that dark skin of yours. Seriously, where the hell did those come from?"

"My mother's eyes were hazel," I told him, smiling as I thought of her.

"It's funny," he said softly, still looking at me. "I bet if you weren't so scary looking that you'd have women all over you all the time."

We never talked about who I'd want all over me, so he had no idea I was gay just like he was. He and I might have the conversation someday, but it wasn't necessary at the moment.

Trevan was first on the elevator, and I turned to face the room, my back to him, as the doors whooshed shut in front of me.

Halfway down, he put his hand on my shoulder. I didn't turn to look at him. I couldn't. I had to be ready if we stopped before we reached the bottom.

"Did you hear him? I'm out," he said excitedly.

"I heard him."

He sucked in a breath. "I want to talk to you."

"Hold on," I cautioned, reaching in my pocket to use my audio scrambler before nodding. "G'head."

"Promise me," he insisted.

"Promise you what?"

"That everything will be okay."

"It will."

"You're positive? I mean, I'm not trying to second-guess you or—"

"I know." I did. He trusted me in all things.

"I'm just worried. "

I was aware.

"You're sure my mother and everyone else will be safe here even if I go with you to Boston."

"Oh, you're going to Boston regardless," I said implacably. "We agreed, and I already put first and last months' rent down on the brownstone on Newbury Street for Landry's business. It's got a nice two-bedroom apartment on the second floor complete with hardwood floors and lots of natural light that Landry will love and a small terrace that you can sit out on."

He sighed deeply. "It sounds awesome, but you didn't have to do—"

"I did. It was my idea for you guys to move to Boston with me, so I had to put my money where my mouth is."

"Yeah, but you're not responsible for me and Landry."

"The hell I'm not."

Trevan was quiet for a moment. "You haven't told me what your new job is."

"I know."

"You didn't—I mean, you didn't take it just because you wanted to protect us, did you?"

"Not only, no. But you and Landry were a consideration."

"But you made the decision mostly for you, right?"

"I did. It was time for a change."

"I'm still a little scared to move. I've lived in Detroit my whole life."

"You're going to love Boston, I have no doubt."

He took a deep breath—I heard the inhale behind me. "Okay. No more going back and forth about it. I'll go there with Landry and let you watch over us some more since it seems like something you like to do, and I don't want to deprive you of the pleasure."

"Thank you, that's very thoughtful."

"That's what people say," he assured me. "That Trevan is a thoughtful guy."

I scoffed.

"Can I ask a question?"

"Can I stop you?"

"Probably, yeah, but I know you won't anymore. You've changed so much in the past few years. It's like night and day, actually."

When I first met him, I had been much more closed off, not sure where my boundaries were. I had maybe ten people in the world who could really say they knew me back then, but slowly, over time, my circle grew along with my caring and my patience and my desire to know others. I was still not ready to host a dinner party, and I could kill all conversation in a room if I wasn't careful, but I was less suspicious these days and more apt to give someone the benefit of the doubt. It was new for me.

"Are you safe?"

"Always," I promised.

"Your friends are looking out for you?"

"Yes."

"And you can count on them?"

"I can."

He squeezed my shoulder. "Aren't you ever scared?"

"There's no point."

"To fear?"

"Yes."

"So what, then?"

"Whatever happens will have an effect. You deal with the ripple."

He let me go. "You're amazing."

"No," I said, exhaling slowly as the elevator came to a stop at the lobby. "Just prepared."

The elevator door opened and—really, that many guns trained on me and Trevan was ridiculous. Who did they think we were?

"I take it back," Trevan gasped from behind me. "This—*this* is overkill."

He wasn't wrong.

"Jesus," Trevan gasped, bumping me from behind, clasping the back of my overcoat.

"Calm yourself," I whispered, glancing around for whoever was in charge of the SWAT team in front of us. When I found who I was looking for, only then did I have a moment of... not fear, that wasn't what made me shiver, but of startled recognition. He looked gobsmacked himself.

"Darius?" he rasped as he came up behind a man holding an M-4 assault rifle on me.

I hadn't heard my name from his lips in over sixteen years; it was both comforting and scary at the same time. "Efrem," I greeted the only man I'd ever loved.

We stood there, staring, and all I saw was green. His eyes—I knew them so well, knew every fleck of indigo, how they looked hooded with passion and blazing with anger. It was thrilling and terrifying to face them again.

Trevan peeked out from behind me. "Are we under arrest?"

Even with the gun pointed at me dead center, I could not keep from smiling. Only my days turned out like this. Seriously. Only mine. Good thing I was all about embracing life changes, never fighting them.

"What a weird day," Trevan breathed out behind me.

Again, he was not wrong.

CHAPTER TWO

ELEVEN MONTHS ago, I was walking through the Tivoli Gardens in Copenhagen in early May. No one who knew me would have ever thought to look for me there; it was basically a family amusement park, after all, so I was surprised when an old friend suddenly appeared. She was standing beside one of the lampposts in the year-round Christmas market and waved during the moment it took me to realize who I was seeing.

"Sello?" I said hoarsely, stunned and wary at the same time. In my business, surprise visits from old friends could be less than welcome.

"What are you doing here?" she asked, her face screwed up with distaste.

"I love it here," I replied, almost defensive. "It's so festive."

She grimaced, panning around, taking in the strings of light, hanging lanterns, decorated spruce trees, and stalls filled with food and ornaments.

"It's even better close to Christmas when the snow is on the ground," I sighed. "It's like walking in a winter wonderland."

"You're not kidding."

"They've got really good rides too."

"Are you reliving your childhood?" she asked as a small crowd of people walked between us. Neither of us had taken a step toward the other.

"It's comforting," I assured her.

"It's terrifying," she corrected, gesturing around her.

"They have an amazing gingerbread shop," I offered cheerfully.

She squinted at me.

"How about a waffle cone?"

"No, thank you."

"Roller coaster?"

She took a step closer and I took one back.

"Why did you do that?"

"Why are you here?" I asked pointedly, crossing my arms as I looked at her, letting her know I was tense, ready, but not opening my coat, not reaching for the Beretta 92FS Combat pistol in my shoulder holster.

"Oh," she said suddenly, like a thought just hit her. "I'm not here to kill you," she announced, looking right, then left at the milling crowd. "Not that I could. Is this why you like it here? You feel safe?"

I nodded. As much as the historic buildings, lush scenery, and immaculately maintained gardens soothed me, the fact that it was a world-class amusement park packed wall to wall with people was a great way to walk around and not worry.

"So, may I speak to you?"

"About?"

She pointed at me. "May I come over there?"

I wasn't sure, still studying her, seeing nothing at all that pinged of danger. She seemed happy to see me and a bit anxious like she was chomping at the bit to deliver some news.

"Please. It's important."

I knew Sello Mogale from when I was with the CIA serving with the South African National Defense Force. We bonded quickly because she liked that I was sarcastic and outspoken and, in her words, kind of an ass. I'd been drawn to her because she was smart, funny, kind, and above all, exceedingly competent. It was not every day one found people who knew what they were doing and excelled at their job. Whenever I encountered those individuals, I tried really hard to keep them in my orbit. I considered Sello a friend and knew she felt the same.

But even though we were, in fact, friendly, she still could have been paid to murder me.

"You're positive you don't have an ice pick that you're going to shove into the back of my head?" I called over.

A few people walking by with their kids cast me glances of pure horror, and Sello's face scrunched up in similar disgust.

"What?" I asked, still keeping my distance.

"You're revolting."

"It's a logical question."

"If you say so," she said with a slight tremble.

"So you're really here just to talk, not to shiv me?"

"Shiv you?" she repeated, horrified.

I chuckled.

"Are you done?"

My grin made her smile in return.

"I'll come over there," I acquiesced, joining her beside the lamppost that looked newer than the 160 years the park had been open. Gazing at her bistre skin with teak-and-gold undertones, I smiled as her warm gaze flitted over me.

"First things first," she began, her voice soft but resonant running through me. "Should I call you something other than the name I know?"

I had a lot of names.

Darius Hawthorne was on my birth certificate.

Terrence Moss was born when I turned nine, after my parents were killed in a home invasion. Then I was moved to Detroit from Bloomfield Hills.

I was sent to live with Emile and Vanessa Moss. At the time, I didn't understand why I had to have a new name, but once I was older and appreciated what witness protection was, it all became clear.

My mother, an assistant district attorney, rolled over on her boss, who was accused of and indicted on bribery charges. Once she testified, she had a giant target on her back, and between her and my father, a successful real estate broker, they were easy to find. It took only a bit of digging years later with the right clearances to find out that they were murdered. So when I was the only member of the Hawthorne family still breathing, I was rechristened Terrence Moss and started over in a big city. It had been strange—and when Vanessa left Emile, even weirder—but he and I coped with it, and in the end, he'd changed for the better. I'd been sad when he died, wondering if I'd ever have a family again.

After I graduated from high school, I joined the Army and moved up through the ranks, becoming first a Ranger, then a Pathfinder. I changed my name again once I left the military and took up with the CIA. Ten years later, at forty-five, I'd built a deadly and dependable reputation as Conrad Harris.

"It depends," I said. "What am I here to discuss? A business proposal or something else?"

"Business," she assured me.

"Then please, Conrad Harris it is."

"Excellent," she sighed. "Now tell me, Conrad, have you ever heard of the vault?"

I had heard it whispered about, mentioned offhand by people who didn't know and glossed over quickly by people who I thought maybe did. "I have a very vague idea," I told her.

"Tell me."

"I think it's some giant warehouse of things that no one wants found."

"Not exactly," Sello replied as she slipped her gloved hand around my bicep, pulling on me gently so I would stroll casually beside her, in step. "The vault is not a place. It's an individual who keeps safe the secrets and possessions, and even the whereabouts of others, for some of the most powerful people on the planet."

"Really? It's not a huge underground bunker where things are kept."

"No, it's not."

"It's a person."

"Yes. It's an office, like any other position."

"And this person, this vault, knows where things are."

"Knows where people are, things, all manner of secrets."

I grinned at her. "Like what?"

"Whatever you can imagine," she admitted. "There are things hidden all over the world, some in the most obscure places and some in plain sight. The vault, and only the vault, is given the key code that makes finding them possible."

"Why tell me?"

"Why do you think?"

I shook my head. "Enough with the cloak-and-dagger bullshit. Just explain to me what the hell's going on."

"Why do you think I would come here and talk to you about all this?"

"I have no idea?"

"Oh?" One eyebrow lifted skeptically. "You have no more imagination than that?"

Letting go of her arm, I rounded on her. "I can imagine all kinds of things, but what this could logically be makes no sense."

"Speak your mind," she prodded, her eyes gleaming in the dusky light. "What do you think I'm doing here?"

I shook my head.

"Come on, hypothesize with me."

Taking a quick breath I said, "You want me to be part of the vault's team and—"

Her cackle made me stop, but my scowl sent her into peals of laughter.

I knew better. No one was going to trust an ex-CIA operative to take part in a team that, from the little I knew, worked internationally. Everyone connected to the vault I'd ever heard whispered about had no ties to the United States.

"I'll see you around," I muttered under my breath, ready to walk away from her.

She grabbed my arm to stop me and then took hold of the lapels of my topcoat. "I'm telling you about the vault because you've been nominated to take the position."

It took a long moment as I listened to the sounds of the park around me: the movement of the crowd as it flowed by, the distant sounds of excited screams from the rollercoasters, and the squeals of children closer as toys and treats were lavished on them.

"Are you listening to me?"

I dropped my head to meet her eyes.

"It's you. You're going to be the next vault."

I DID not take the news well. She used the time that I was gobsmacked and lost in confusion to steer me out of the amusement park and into a cab.

"What the hell are you talking about?" I railed when my voice and brain were finally back online. "And where the hell are we going?"

"We're going to have dinner at Geranium," she announced. "I always tell myself I'll eat there when I'm here in Copenhagen, but I never get the chance."

"Too busy killing people?" I baited.

"Yes," she replied drolly. "My schedule is always so cluttered with murder that I never get to have dinner."

I grunted as she leaned forward to tell the driver we were going to Denmark's national soccer stadium in the center of the city. From his chuckle, I understood that he knew exactly where the restaurant was, and he didn't need her to give him the location.

I ignored her as she sat back, wedged beside me instead of giving me space, even though I was aware she was staring at my profile.

"You would be the first US citizen to head the organization," she informed me. It felt out of the blue to me, but I could tell from her expression of almost boredom that she thought we were continuing our conversation.

I didn't bite.

Heavy sigh from her. "Would you like to know how the vault is chosen?"

I finally turned.

"Every vault chooses their successor," she explained slowly, carefully. "The name is given, that person vetted, and then, if the choice meets the criteria—"

"Which is what?"

"Military background, leadership skills—freelance as well as associated operative—fluency in at least six languages, but more than all of that, a person with the respect of the community at large."

"And what community is that?"

"You know which one that is."

And I did, the global one of professional contractors. "You're saying I was chosen."

"Yes."

I wasn't ready to get to the rest; there were more important questions first. "What happened to the last vault?"

"We lost her ten days ago in a car bombing in Tehran."

"Someone came after her because she was the vault?"

"No. No one knew who she was in our organization; she was killed because she was a woman of power in Iran."

I nodded. There were still so many men threatened by women, and though I'd never been one of them myself, I'd known my fair share. "I'm sorry you lost her."

"As were we. Zineb Faris was excellent, and we were sorry to lose her."

"I knew her," I said, surprised. "Zineb. I worked with her when I was lent out to the Republican Guard five years ago. She made Egypt bearable."

The woman I'd known had been fearless. I remembered eating dinner out with her in Cairo, and on the way back to the hotel, her long brown-black hair falling around her, we'd been jumped by men who would have been reported as street thugs but who were really highly trained extremists who did not want her there trying her damndest, along with her team, to work toward a united Egypt. Of the six who came after us, she took down five alone, and when she was done, she'd asked if I wanted a drink.

"She was funny," I said.

"Yes, she was."

We both went silent for a few minutes as we reached the soccer stadium. Once outside on the street, Sello took my arm and steered me into the building. Up eight floors with people who worked there getting on and off the elevator, we reached the restaurant and had to suspend our conversation as we were warmly greeted by the hostess, who took our jackets before introducing us to one of the chefs, who came to take us on a tour of the open-concept kitchen, some other smaller preparation areas, and the massive wine cellar. The view of the stadium was impressive, and from our table we had a view of a massive park.

Once seated, we met our server, who explained about our meal, and while I zoned out, Sello listened and asked questions. I was about to interrupt and ask for a drink, but Sello shushed me, to the delight of our server, who turned and left.

"What was that?"

"I want you clearheaded," she informed me, "so we're both having the juice pairing instead of the wine."

"You're kidding," I groused.

"I'm not, and I understand it's amazing, so stop fretting."

"I don't fret," I clarified coolly, making myself understood.

The condescending look she gave me let me know precisely what she thought of me.

"You know," I said, leaning forward, elbows down. "It doesn't sound like the vault is such a great position to have if they can be killed off so easily."

"It's not easy," she assured me, hands laced on the table. "The vault in fact has their own team, but you know as well as I do, if someone truly wants you dead, and they're willing to trade their life for yours—there's very little to be done to deter that sort of madness."

It was true; I'd sadly seen it happen many times in my life.

"I liked her," I breathed.

Sello smiled. "As did I. The position was safe in her hands, and normally there is concern from at least one quarter."

"So you're saying everyone was comfortable with her."

"She had a strength about her."

"Yes."

I regarded her for a moment. "You know not everyone would be comfortable with a man like me taking the helm."

She squinted at me. "I'll have to disagree, because when your name was reported to us by her bishop, everyone agreed you were an excellent choice."

"Is that right?"

"Yes," she said firmly, as though I'd argued the point adamantly instead of with only a trace of sarcasm. "When we convened to agree on the transfer of power, there was not one person who disagreed with your nomination after reading your dossier."

"And that nomination came to you through Zineb's 'bishop.'"

She nodded instead of explaining as the waitress placed a wine glass in front of me.

"I thought you said we were having juice," I said to Sello.

"And you thought what, they'd serve it in a tumbler?"

I had, actually. "You used this meeting as an excuse to eat at this restaurant."

She nodded cheerfully. "I thought I said that already."

I was quiet as a vegetable dish was served, and while it tasted incredible and I enjoyed it, watching Sello experience it was almost as good. "You didn't think I was too dangerous to bring here?"

Her glare made me smile. "All your life you've adhered to a code," she reminded me, her eyes taking me in. "I don't expect you to become ruthless with me."

She had a point.

I took a breath, breathed in the intoxicating smells in the restaurant, gazed out the window at the incredible view, and then returned my attention to my companion.

"All settled in your skin now?"

I was.

"Drink your juice."

I waited until the second course of appetizers arrived to start talking to her again. "What is this?"

"Isn't it gorgeous," she sighed, utterly in awe of what was on her plate.

I had to give it to her "Yes. It's art. I don't know if I can eat this, I'd feel bad."

The waitress was still there and chuckled at me. "First you see it, find it beautiful, and then you experience the flavors," she educated me. "The chef would be heartbroken if you didn't enjoy his food."

The Jerusalem artichoke leaves, walnut oil, and rye vinegar looked amazing, and though it resembled a display in a high-end florist, the whole thing was edible.

"I think I want to live here," Sello let me know.

"It's too pretty to eat," I agreed.

She smiled at me. "All right, ask your questions."

"What's a bishop?"

"The bishop is the vault's second," she explained. "They're the person who holds the key code after the vault dies until it can be passed to the new vault."

"And this bishop, you're trusting them to not break this bond?

"Yes."

"And what if the bishop kills the vault for their key code?"

"That could never happen."

"Why not?"

She tipped her head to scrutinize me. "The bishop is someone who would never break faith with the vault. They are their closest advisor, their—"

"Friend." I finished for her.

"Oh no," she said quickly, brows furrowing. "The bishop is a soldier, a trusted ally, but not a friend."

"Because?"

"A friend might get angry with you, feel that they have reason to bear a grudge, and change alliances. A soldier does not make those choices; they support loyalty, the defense of another, the guardianship of another. I'm speaking of the sacred trust between master and servant, where the master shelters the servant and provides a life, and the servant protects and stands between his master and the world."

I understood what she meant. I'd been both in my life.

"So that's why when Zineb's bishop brought you my name, there was never any question that it was the truth."

"No," she said, receiving her charred potato from the kitchen. It was a single potato, a single bite, and though it looked like a round charcoal briquette, it tasted like heaven. The teaspoon of sheep's butter that accompanied it was fabulous as well. "I'm going to have to bring my husband," she said with a sigh.

To have her, in the midst of all this, so excited about food gave me hope. The simple pleasures in life, like eating great food, were still cause for bliss.

"On Zineb's word," I began, because I needed to be certain, "you're going to pass the position of the vault to me."

"Yes."

"Because that's what you do."

"We do the background checks, but you were, or course, already on our radar, so it was simply a matter of pulling up your dossier and verifying that you were in fact, still alive."

"That's a good point. What if the person the vault wants is dead?"

"Then we look to the teams of the vault and evaluate."

"Teams?"

"The vault has two teams. The first is the guild, which belongs to the doors—except for their team leader, the bishop, who is handpicked by you."

"From a list of your people?"

"No. That person is designated by you. He, or she, is your vassal, if you will, your person, and they manage the retrieval team as your bishop—that's what the position is called—and they belong to you but lead our team."

"So this is the person doing all the traveling."

"Yes and no. They direct the team that collects the items or people being placed into your care."

"It's basically a management position."

"I prefer to think of the bishop as being more of a liaison between the vault and us, the doors, officially Global Research and Development," she corrected, "and the team and you."

"And the other team?"

"The other team, the court, is exclusively yours, and—"

"Guild and court," I said, chuckling. "Really?"

"They're not my names. The vault is a centuries-old position. I suspect that the men who created this international agency originally were trying for simple."

"Sure," I agreed. "Go on."

"Well, the court, the doors have nothing to do with at all. They are your people, not to exceed five, who specifically protect you. Then we protect those you declare to us, as required."

"Required?"

"You are allowed to choose ten people—family members or friends—who will be protected with our considerable resources until the vault's death."

"Why not for their entire lives?"

"If the vault dies, the people they love don't need protection anymore. Why would they?"

"It's like witness protection."

"Yes." She said liking the comparison, taking a moment to coo over the food that came and went, the appetizers arriving at perfect intervals.

"If the guy who could point the finger is dead, everyone else in his or her family is off the hook."

"Precisely."

I scoffed. "So let me understand. The doors protect those ten people that I would give you the names of, but not me."

"Correct. Not you. You're responsible for your own protection. That's what the court is for."

"Explain."

"Only a handful of people know the identity of the vault. We protect the people on your list purely for your benefit and in case you slip up and disclose who you are. No one wants to see the vault pressured into giving up secrets."

"Right."

"We protect your people, and your handpicked team protects you."

"Five people on my team?"

"Yes, and one of them, your knight, must be on your master list of those we protect. There has to be an overlap between the two teams."

"Why?"

"So someone will be left standing to report back to us in case we lose you."

"I thought the bishop did that."

"They do, but if somehow, the bishop is killed as well, then the last person standing is the knight."

"The key code then goes from the bishop to the knight."

"In extreme circumstances, yes," she agreed solemnly, her expression concerned. "But we've never had that happen in over a hundred years."

I already knew who I was going to tap to be my knight, the guy watching my back. I would put his name on the list, and it would be done. I really hoped he was still in Boston. It would be damn annoying if he was dead.

I wanted Ceaton Mercer to be my knight. The first time I laid eyes on him, he was an Army sniper. Soon after that, he'd been discharged for not following orders, but those orders would have left me and my team unprotected in a war zone. Though I had been unsuccessful in saving his career, I would now be able to return the favor and get him out of the life of crime he currently found himself in. He'd fallen on hard times and went to work for Grigor Jankovic, head of the Serbian mob in Boston. I had no doubt that even though Ceaton was not doing what I would have wanted for him, he was still a good man with a conscience. If I needed him, I had no doubt I could present a compelling enough argument to get him. I could be quite persuasive when I put my mind to it.

"Conrad?"

"Sorry," I said quickly as fjord shrimp lightly smoked in juniper, lumpfish roe, and oyster soup was set down in front of me.

"Did you hear what I asked."

"No."

Her smile was kind. "I need your answer. Will you take the job?"

"You think it's that simple?"

"It is."

I searched her face. "You actually want me to decide right this second?"

"I do."

"Yes, but—"

"Why do you hesitate? You accept only the occasional contract these days, you're not active with the company as a freelancer anymore, and from what I can tell, you've been in Detroit providing protection to a low-level gun runner. What's stopping you?"

"Oh, I don't know, perhaps the enormity of the task?"

She waved her hand dismissively. "You're ridiculously overqualified, and if the court you choose is anything like you, I'm excited to see what you can do in the job. What you could grow it into."

I scowled.

"You already have people in mind, don't you?"

I wasn't about to tell her I was already excited about the new opportunity open to me. I'd been floating along for so long, to have a solid purpose would be more than welcome. "It seems like a lot of work for one person," I grumbled.

"It's not only one person," she corrected. "It's a whole network of people."

"You mentioned doors."

"I did. Let me explain."

I listened as she explained that the vault was the overseer of an international group of people called doors, like openings to be walked through, going deeper and deeper toward an inner sanctum until finally reaching the center: the vault. All these individuals reported to the vault—never knowing the real identity of their boss—collected objects, data, people, substances, any and all things the vault agreed to take in. They were intermediaries for transactions and nothing more.

"They go by the name Global Research and Development. All those people would report to your bishop."

"And who are you?"

"You mean 'me' as in those who would place you in the position of the vault?"

"Yes."

"We're a cartel, an organization like any other, except we don't do anything but facilitate the operation of the vault."

"So you all have no day-to-day interaction with the doors or the bishop or me and my protection team headed by the knight. You only work when there's no vault."

"Precisely."

"So, then what, you all have day jobs?"

She nodded, happily digging into the plate of pickled carrots, smoked pork fat, and melted vesterhavs cheese set in front of her.

"This whole operation, then, Global Research and Development, that's just a front for the vault."

I received no answer, just her eyes closed, head back—she was clearly lost in the complete and utter joy of gourmet food.

"Sello?"

I'd had no idea how there could be twenty courses that took almost four hours to eat, but I understood once I saw the portions. They were small but perfect, and she was over the moon with her meal and juice. My company had very little to do with her current happiness.

"I'm so glad you're here with me," she said, her gorgeous dark liquid sepia eyes drifting open. "It would only be better were my husband here."

As compliments went, it was a good one. "Why is that?"

"You have a very solid, quiet way about you that's terribly comforting, your voice is a silky rumble that's quite sexy and soothing at the same time, and you're very nice to look at."

"Yes, well, you too," I replied gruffly.

She beamed at me. "Now, to your point, there is no day-to-day contact between us, those who put the vault in place, and you. Once you're on the throne, as it were, we leave you alone. All of it, the mechanics of the job, are on you, your bishop, and your knight."

"I need an example of how things work."

"All right," she agreed, her long fingers delicately lifting her wine glass filled with juice. "Give me a hypothetical."

I thought of my friend Duncan Stiel and what he'd asked me to do. "Okay, let's say someone asks me to keep a gun."

I'd been in Chicago on a job, finishing up some reconnaissance for Javier Aranda. He'd wanted to make sure a friend of his was safe, so I shadowed the doctor who'd saved his mother. I'd debated killing the man on general principle, but just because I could, didn't mean I should, so instead I reported in that he was safe and well. I was on my way back to Detroit when Duncan called.

We met at Three Happiness, our favorite dim sum place down on Cermak, and sat there talking over beers until he carded his fingers through his thick dirty blond hair one too many times.

"For God's sake, what's wrong?" I asked my childhood friend.

We'd been friends since the fifth grade, when I went into WITSEC. Years later, the past hardly mattered, only the fact that we'd reconnected when I was done being a CIA operative and could step back into my life.

As soon as I could see him, I did. I couldn't tell him where I'd been for many years after we joined the Army together, and he'd never asked. I was certain he assumed the worst—I'd been a mercenary or something worse—but that was better than the alternative. I enjoyed being back in his life, even if we didn't see each other as much as I'd like. The best part was that I finally could give him my number, and he was using it.

Simple changes in my life like that were good.

He still wasn't answering me, so I leaned forward and wrapped my hand loosely around his wrist. "Duncan?"

"I have a gun I need to get rid of, T."

He'd always known me as Terrence Moss, and I'd never corrected him. "That all?"

His head snapped up. "I just—I'm never alone, and I can't tell Aaron." He choked. "He thinks I'm a good guy."

"You *are* a good guy."

"I'm getting rid of a gun for someone."

"Who?"

"That's the worst of it," he said sadly. "I'm doing it to protect my ex."

I had to think. "Your ex was a college professor, wasn't he?"

"Yeah."

"Nate something?"

"Quells, yeah, but his husband killed the guy who tried to kill Nate."

"And did what with the gun?"

"Ditched it in a sewer."

"And let me guess, someone else saw him."

"Yeah."

I nodded. "Where do you come in?"

"The gun came across my desk with a lot of others being transferred to the Justice Department, and once I saw what case it was attached to—I made sure it didn't leave."

"You know," I said, grinning at him, "that's really idiotic."

He groaned loudly.

"Where's the gun now?"

"In my glove compartment."

I snorted.

"What?"

"You've been just driving around with it."

"I told you, I'm never alone."

"Why call me?"

He took a breath. "I needed to tell someone I could trust."

And when I looked at his face, in his eyes, I knew the truth. He had not called me to fix this; he only wanted to share his secret before he exploded.

"Here's what we're going to do," I began. "When we're done eating, we're going to walk outside together, and you're going to give me the gun."

"What?" He was surprised. I heard it in his voice, with the relief and shame.

"Yes."

"Fuck no," he yelled, getting up. "That is not what this was about. I didn't call you to—"

"I know," I soothed. "Sit down."

He sat.

"I have very few friends," I explained flatly, taking hold of his shoulder. "Let me do this."

"My intention was not—"

"Stop." I shut him down. "Listen to me, just this once."

"I—"

"I have something to tell you."

He took a breath. "G'head."

"I don't want you to call me Terrence anymore."

He squinted, and I explained, and after he took a few long minutes to absorb the news, I saw the smile I was hoping for. "So you're going to use the new name and give me the weapon."

And after a moment, with his gunmetal eyes on mine, he nodded silently. We didn't talk anymore about it.

Sello broke into my thoughts. "The vault would never take a gun," she said. "Many guns, yes. Enough to use in a revolution, certainly. But not a single pistol or rifle or whatever."

"What if it was a weapon that proved someone's guilt or innocence?"

"The vault would be given a person if he or she were important enough, but not a gun that would incriminate them."

"So the vault takes in people and does what? Protects them? It's like witness protection?"

"No, it's like being erased. People are remade through surgery, documentation, and other available resources. That person basically dies and there is no record of them."

"Like I did," I said matter-of-fact. "After I left the Army and went to work for the company."

"Yes, but you still have your own face," she pointed out. "Someone who knew you twenty years ago could still pass you on the street and know whatever name you went by the last time they saw you."

"You're saying people given to the vault are unmade and then remade."

"Yes. That's what I'm saying."

"How does the vault police its contents?"

"The doors, again. They keep the records of everything."

"And how is that hackproof?"

"The best hackers in the world work for the vault, and we pay them what they're worth. They understand their value, as do we."

It made sense. "Give me an example of how items in the vault are tracked."

She thought a moment. "A year ago, two men who had placed items with the vault needed to withdraw them so they could make an exchange."

"I hesitate to ask."

"One was a lost Van Gogh, the other was VX gas."

Jesus.

"The man making the purchase wanted to decimate a small town in Yemen."

I remained stoic, not letting her see how much that scenario terrified me.

"The vault made the exchange, so everyone could see and hear that the vault merely facilitated the transaction, and all was well."

"But what really happened?"

"The vault killed the man who bought the gas, making it look like an accident, and then killed the man who sold the gas and made it look like it was from natural causes."

"It wasn't suspicious, them dying so soon afterwards?"

Sello shrugged. "Things happen all the time, especially in our business."

"True."

"It looked like the vault did what was asked without any repercussions. Only we know what really happened."

"Then the vault is, in fact, a watchdog."

"Yes, one now presently in possession of a lovely Van Gogh and several canisters of VX gas."

"What you're telling me is that basically, the vault plays God."

"Yes."

I took a breath. "The hubris is incredible."

"It is and isn't," she apprised me. "What makes these choices any different than a general's during wartime? What makes that any different from any man—or woman—who commands troops? Can that not be said of any leader throughout history?"

There was that.

"How is that decision any different from any other life and death one?"

It wasn't, she was right.

"Eat your food," she ordered, pointing at the morels, sunflower seeds, and truffles on the plate that had just been delivered to the table.

"Are there seriously twenty courses?"

She grinned as she nodded. "There were eight appetizers alone."

"With all the dishes coming and going from the table, this might not have been the best place in the world for us to have this talk."

"Perhaps not, but you have to live life to the fullest," she informed me, a bit high-handed, "and really, no one is going to listen in on our conversation."

"No, I know, but—"

"And for the record, these ethical quandaries that you're grilling me about—oh dear Lord, that's amazing." She whimpered over the food. "Those instances of having to choose what's right are few and far between."

"Why?"

"Well, because most people who contact the vault do so quietly, secretly, not wanting to alert another living soul as to their plans."

"And why is that?"

"Because it's either for personal gain or they're working against time and are scared to death of the consequences."

"You're saying that in most instances, someone is entrusting the vault with something that will save their own life."

"Yes," she agreed. "We don't have weapons of mass destruction. I'm not saying that we would never—that's a ridiculous statement to even contemplate—but what we have is a lot of diaries, written correspondence, photographs, a server full of deleted correspondence, and gems. Our collection of precious stones rivals any museum's in the world."

"Because money is more easily transacted in that form."

"Yes."

"Is there a central place where items are housed?"

"No. Things are kept in giant impenetrable safes in banks in Switzerland and in plain sight in people's homes. Only the vault has the key code which unlocks the master list."

"What you're basically telling me is that only the vault knows where the bodies are buried."

"Precisely."

"How is it done?"

"That's a very broad question."

It was. "Tell me, how do people use the vault? How does anyone know what's in there, and how do they contact the vault to begin with?

She grimaced. "My answer is going to sound very prosaic. There's a website."

It took me a minute.

"I told you."

"You're kidding."

She shook her head.

"A website."

A quick nod and a wince, like she knew it was ridiculous.

"Don't tell me," I said sarcastically. "If you search for Global Research and Development, that's the website."

"Yes," she acceded with a shrug. "One navigates to the website and there's a single box where you enter the item you want placed in the vault."

"That's the stupidest thing I ever heard."

"It's not stupid, it just lacks grandeur and imagination."

I shook my head. "What did they have before the Internet?"

"Letters," she disclosed, scowling at me as though I was the one with the ridiculous answers. "That seems obvious."

"You know you should be—"

"I wonder if they would give me the recipe for this currant juice," she asked me.

"No, they won't," I said, just to be a wet blanket. "Now, what if someone wants to know if an item is in the vault? Is there a search function on the website?"

She chuckled. "After a fashion, dear. If you know the name of the item, for example, Stalin's diary—"

I couldn't stifle my gasp.

"It's an example," she chided.

"Ah."

"You could also search by the name of a person, and if there is anything remotely relating to Stalin that is a ledger, diary, journal, anything like that, then the entire screen becomes green to let you know that the item is, in fact, with the vault."

"So you can check to see if the vault has something."

"Absolutely, and people do, every day."

"Really?"

"Yes. Last year there was a drug cartel head's daughter who spent three days on the site asking for things like the gun that Jack Ruby used to kill Lee Harvey Oswald with."

"Isn't that gun in a museum somewhere?"

"I have no idea, but we certainly don't have it."

I grunted.

"She asked for alien spaceship pieces and parts of Amelia Earhart's plane."

"Okay, I get it."

Sello thanked the chef, who came to our table to explain the pork, pickled young garlic, pine and black currants leaves that we had next. Everyone was so gracious that even being interrupted was not annoying.

"There are specifics I can share with you if that's what you want," she assured me once we were alone. "Is that what you want?"

I wasn't sure what I wanted. "Tell me the way it works."

"First you need special software to find the site. This isn't on Google, you understand."

"The dark net."

"Yes."

"All right."

"You find the site, and once there people type in what they would like to place with the vault. The doors monitor the site, of course, seeing all activity, knowing precisely who is online and has access to registration at all times."

"Go on."

"The doors funnel the requests to the vault, who then agrees to or denies the request."

"That seems like a lot of work."

"Not really, not that part of the process."

"Why not? The requests must be in the thousands."

"Oh, no, not at all."

"No?"

"You have to think about it logically. Most of the powerful people in the world are also ridiculously well off, so they have their own protocols, their own safes, and their own places to hide their dirty little secrets. The only people who reach out to the vault don't want to have daily access to whatever it is they need to have protected."

"Sure."

"They're throwing something down a well, as it were."

I nodded.

"So the number of people who actually contact us is between ten to twenty a day."

"Really."

"Yes. It's not like the return line at Target the day after Christmas."

I chuckled. "Retail frightens you, does it?"

Her eyes widened. "The mall is terrifying."

"I can't say I've been."

"No kids?" she asked.

"No."

Quick nod. "Well, believe me when I tell you, there is not a lot of traffic on the site."

"But what there is, is life and death."

"It is, that's true."

"And so where do you come in, precisely?"

"As I said, once the transfer is made, we disband until the time comes for a new vault to be chosen."

I absorbed that. "May I ask, why not have someone within your organization become the vault? Why let Zineb choose and whoever before her?"

She shook her head. "It has to be someone neutral, it can't be anyone who knows that this is planned for them." She said with a deep sigh of contentment as the last plate was taken away. "It must also be someone well acquainted with death."

"Someone who's killed for a living," I said implacably.

"Yes," she agreed, leaning forward to put her hand on mine. "Many of the people who come together to manage the process of the transfer of power have never been in the field and have no idea what taking a life feels like."

"And it's important to you that the vault knows that," I stated.

"Yes. The vault is responsible for saying yes and no, and if you've never been responsible for a life, for taking one or not, how can your decisions be truly informed?"

It made sense.

"Well," she said brightly, "we're about to have dessert and coffee, and it will take another hour at least, and we have to move from the table, so… do you want to wait until that's done, or would you like to give me an answer now?"

I stared at her face.

"Well? May I tell the others that you've accepted your fate?"

"Really? This is my fate?"

"Isn't it? I mean, truly, what else are you going to do with yourself?"

She had a point.

CHAPTER THREE

NOW, SIX months after making Ceaton Mercer my knight and living my new life as the vault, I was working on getting Trevan Bean and his husband out of Detroit in one piece, so, of course, this was the time I was suddenly faced with my ex, Homeland Security Agent Efrem Lahm. At the moment, he was pacing in front of a steel table in one of the many interrogation rooms at the Office of Homeland Security down on Fort Street, where he brought us after the police turned us over to his custody.

I had no clue where Trevan was, but that was all right. He wasn't in any danger. This wasn't some frightening rendition of a situation with my ex, and even if it was, I could count on my bishop to get me out.

"Explain yourself!" he roared.

The outburst was surprising, not because of the volume, but the intensity.

"Darius!"

I smiled. I couldn't help it. He caught me when he turned. "Sorry."

Moving fast, he slammed both hands on the table and loomed over me. "What the hell is so funny?"

I shook my head. "Nothing's funny, it's just nice."

"*Nice?*" he demanded, the outrage clear in his voice, beside himself with anger, indignation, and confusion.

"Yeah, nice," I said, looking up into his face. I would have reached for him if my hands weren't shackled to the top of the table. "Just happy to see you."

Efrem was angry: I could hear the sharpness in his voice and the snarl, see the fury spilled across his features in the clenching of his jaw, the cording of the muscles in his neck, and the furrow of his golden brows. With the twitch in his left cheek and the splotchy flush on his throat, he looked like his brain was going to explode. Of course, none of that detracted from how drop-dead gorgeous he'd become. I'd thought he was pretty when he was in his midtwenties—the last time I saw him—but at forty-three, he was blinding.

His frame that had once been thin and rangy was now more filled out, resembling a swimmer's body with long, lean muscles, broad shoulders, and a chest I wanted to get my hands on. His coloring was the same, the light golden tan I knew from past experience covered his entire body. As usual, though, what mesmerized me were his eyes and the sharp, defined angles of his face, the light golden stubble, his long lashes, and the curve of his mouth. I squirmed in my seat, surprised I was having such a visceral reaction to being close to him but also aware that this *was* Efrem, after all. I had never stopped wanting him, loving him.

"Where have you been?" he asked, his voice cracking at the end, making him sound heartbroken in the midst of what was supposed to be an interrogation about why Trevan and I were in the home of Marc Eastman.

I would have thought he'd forgotten me after a little over sixteen years. I'd been very careful to never look for him before my circumstances changed.

Even before I became the vault, with my security clearance and the traveling I did, I'd had the power to find out where he was, then arrange to run into him on the street or when he turned a corner. Or I could have just been wherever he was when he walked in the door at the end of the day. I killed people for a living. It was my job. Most of the time it had been for my government, in the name of democracy and being the safety net of the world. I committed those murders to prevent bigger crime with a much higher body count... most of the time. But I also killed when it was necessary to make sure my friends were secure. It didn't happen often—I didn't have that many friends—but no one asked what I did when I wasn't on the clock, and I didn't volunteer anything. Everyone had plausible deniability that way.

But none of that mattered at the moment, because Efrem Lahm was waiting for answers.

"Answer me!"

I cleared my throat. "I never looked for you."

Several ticks of the clock went by.

"I just wanted you to know that, so we're clear." I needed him to understand that I had not, and would never, interfere in his life.

More silence, until "What?"

"I don't want you to think I was stalking you or anything."

The muscles in his jaw twitched again. "I'm sorry?"

"I never went near you."

"I've missed a step."

I cleared my throat. "I could have found you, but I didn't want to just show up out of the blue. I didn't want to create any complication in your life."

Again there was a lull.

"I would never have intruded," I explained. "You get that, right?"

"Intrude?"

"On your life," I repeated, and then it occurred to me to ask, "Are you listening?"

"So you stayed away on purpose?" he clarified.

"Of course," I replied.

He took a breath, and I saw him grip the edge of the table.

"Are you all right?"

It took him a moment to collect himself, and I watched a deluge of emotions chase themselves across his chiseled patrician features and cloud the normally limpid green gaze.

"Ef?" I said, the shortened version of his name coming back that fast. I'd used it for the five years we were together; sixteen apart didn't erase it.

"I— Where—"

"Do you need to sit down?" I asked, worried a bit because of how pale he appeared under the flush that pinked his cheeks. Maybe, just possibly, he was going to puke. "You're not going to hyperventilate, are you?"

"I don't—" he choked out. "I haven't done that in—"

"Do you have an assistant or—"

He shot me a look of annoyance. "You act like you could actually just open the door and get someone in here."

"Well, no," I admitted. "But I could yell for help if you were going to pass out or something."

He opened his mouth to speak.

"But if you could hold on until Lee gets here, that'd be great."

The bracing he did—clenching his jaw, straightening his shoulders, crossing his arms over his chest, opening his stance, planting his feet—was telling.

Still, after all this time, it appeared he was possessive. The behavior, what it looked like on him, had not changed, and I had to admit, it was endearing. I would have missed it had it been gone.

Once when we were on leave in Rome, we'd been out at a club, and a guy sauntered over to where we were holding up the wall and asked if I wanted to dance. Efrem had adopted the same battle stance then as he was now. Clearly he was bothered, and though having him be possessive was a big fat turn-on, I needed to clear this up.

"Lee Tae San works for me," I said.

A scowl darkened his face. "What?"

"You're getting all worked up, which is kind of hot, but I want you to know Lee is my bish—my second, he works for me, that's all."

"Hot?" His voice rose a bit higher than I thought he would have wanted.

I nodded.

"You think—"

"I do," I insisted. "And yeah, you being jealous is crazy hot."

The existing flush didn't slowly creep up his neck and spread to his cheeks. It wasn't that subtle. He turned bright red, and his pupils dilated to big black marbles in seconds.

"I don't care if you have—I mean… I don't care who's coming to get—"

"Yes, you do," I replied with absolute conviction.

"I—what? You can't know that," he protested. "You don't know anything about me! You have no idea how I feel or who I am any—"

I snorted out a laugh.

"Darius!"

For the longest time, before I'd stepped in and taken Ceaton and his crew under my wing, Efrem Lahm would have been the only one who would see me and connect that name with my face. It was nice now that more people knew it, but hearing the first man I'd ever trusted with the name use it again washed me with happiness. I didn't know how much I'd missed hearing that until I started using it again.

I now had all his attention.

"What in the world are you—"

"It's my name."

"I don't—"

"It's because you used to be the only one who used it, and even though you're not anymore... it still means the most coming from you because, for a long time, you were the one and only keeper of that secret."

"Darius—"

"Remember when I told you?"

His eyes searched mine.

I could recall with absolute certainty when I'd told him.

We rented a houseboat from the Antelope Point Marina and took it out on Lake Powell. Everything we needed came with the seventy-five footer: food, too much alcohol, and a fantastic view of the red sandstone cliffs. It was stunning, and between the sparkling clear indigo water, my golden browned man, and the gorgeous pink and purple sunsets every night, I'd taken the plunge and unburdened my soul.

He was out on the deck, stretched out, sipping on the beer I'd given him when he walked by. I stood in the doorway and studied him.

After a moment, he turned to look at me, and the smile I got creased the lines around his eyes, made his dimples pop, and his lips curled dangerously. "Why don't you sit with me?"

I cleared my throat. "I, uhm, need to tell you something."

The smile disappeared instantly, as did the languid recline. He sat up and turned, feet on the deck, waiting.

I smiled slightly. "No, it's not all that. Our vacation hasn't been cancelled."

He released his lungs of air, like he'd been holding it, in greeting my announcement. "Okay, good. I haven't seen you in a month, so I don't want to have to tie you up, but I did come prepared for that possibility."

"Oh, is that right?" I said, chuckling, because it was sexy, yes, that he wanted me, and we were being playful, but mostly it spoke volumes to how much he'd missed me. Not that I wasn't feeling it myself. I had counted the minutes during the last three days of my mission because if nothing came up in seventy-two hours, it normally meant all systems were a go. I could count the vacation as really happening once we hit that mark.

No one was supposed to know, and after the deployment he was just one buddy picking up another from the airport. We had to wait as my team swirled around us, exchanging only pleasantries as we walked through Sky Harbor airport in Phoenix until finally, we were at his car. He'd parked in long-term even though he was just picking me up because there was very little coming in or going out, just us on a stretch of pavement.

He'd rented an enormous Lincoln Navigator with blacked-out windows, and it made no sense until I closed the door and he was on me.

"Come here," he snarled, wrenching me out of my seat and shifting us between them to the folded-over seats he'd already laid flat and covered under a beach blanket. All of them, two rows that could comfortably accommodate seven, were now down, space to be used in whatever way we wanted.

Bumping, jostling, him tugging on my clothes, me trying to get us gently situated was a struggle until we hit the blanketed, uneven backs of the seats, and he rolled me to my back, straddling my thighs.

"You missed me," I stated unnecessarily, reaching for him.

He choked out an answer that was sounds, not words, and dove into my hands, trembling as I slid my fingers over his face, traced along his jaw and his throat and around the back of his neck.

As I eased him down, he opened for me when I kissed him, his moan full of ache and need, completely unselfconscious, trusting me with the knowledge that I had power over him.

"I missed you too," I said between mauling kisses, taking his mouth, making him mine, uncomfortable underneath him, my erection straining against my fatigues.

"I can't do this anymore," he cried out when I let him breathe, the kisses coming one after another, the sensations rolling through me like waves, the rise and fall of surging want. "You have to quit and be home when I get there every night."

I smiled against his lips before I put him on his back, never stopping my assault, letting him take gulps of air between his words.

"I'm rich—my family... I'll take care of you and—Terrence!"

The bite on his throat caused the jolt and the yell, and I took that opportunity to put him on his belly with his ass in the air.

"Rich, huh? How rich?"

He shivered as I slipped off his sneakers before going to work on his belt. "My family owns an oil and gas company in Oklahoma."

"So, a million?" I asked, unsnapping his jeans and getting the zipper down so I could shuck everything, briefs included, first to his knees, and then, after lifting each leg, to his ankles and off.

"More than that," he croaked as I bent and licked over his crease, needing my hands free to loosen up my clothes enough to let my hard, aching shaft bob free.

I'd thrown my duffel behind the front seat, which was lucky. I'd bought lube and put it on top so it would be easy to grab. "Billions?" I offered, keeping him talking as I slid an arm around his chest, settling my weight against his back.

"Not quite billions," he rasped, bucking under me at the sound of the cap snapping open.

One-handed, I squeezed out lube and smeared it on my fingers, coating my cock, the entire length that had in the past been too much for other men. It was too wide, too long—a club, one guy had said, that he knew he could never take in. Others had been all too happy to try, but only Efrem had never made it a thing, simply part of me, a part he craved as much as the rest of me.

"So you want me to do what?" I teased, pressing my slick fingers into his ass, the lube cool, bringing up a deep, lusty moan.

"Just sit around all day and wait for you to come home? Won't I get bored?"

"I… you.…"

"I'm a Ranger, you know. We don't just stay home and garden."

"You can't leave me, and— I can't— T," he whimpered, pushing back, needing my fingers deeper. "What are you doing, just—please."

"You know I will take care of you."

"Yes, I know, always," he agreed, but I heard the soft chanted pleading under his breath. When I notched against him, I promised to go slow.

"You will not," he growled.

I wanted to be gentle. He wasn't about to let me.

As I pressed forward, easing inside just a fraction, my name came out in a slur of garbled sound.

My body shivered with the need to ravish him, to take what I wanted and make him mine. It was primal, and I fought it, instead pushing in slowly, watching his hole stretch around my cock.

"I need you now!" he yelled, and I could hear the frustration and yearning and knew not listening to him was a mistake. If the roles were reversed and he did my thinking for me instead of taking me at my word, instead of trusting him, it might make me wonder if he knew me at all. I would not take the chance of losing him. I would not.

Shoving forward in one long, rough stroke, I buried myself to the balls in his ass.

"Fuck!" he roared.

I froze. "Tell me I didn't hurt—"

"Move, T," he begged, his whole body shuddering under me. "Do it now."

I slipped out, just partially, then shoved back inside, and keening, mewling sounds tumbled out of his throat in response, along with renewed shivering. There was no question about what he wanted, what he had to have.

I had a hand on his hip, anchoring him to me, and the other between his shoulder blades holding him still, keeping him where I wanted him, solid beneath me.

"T," he crooned as I thrust deep and hard into the vise of heat.

"Touch yourself," I ordered, my movements becoming erratic, the snap of my hips getting faster as I had to have more, be *in* him, no more retreat.

I curled over him, kissing his neck, inhaling his scent as I nuzzled in his hair and finally lifted and turned his head to claim his mouth.

Kissing Efrem while I was inside him was my favorite thing in the world. With his heart beating under my palm, his muscles squeezing me tight, milking my length and his tongue rubbing over mine, mirroring the movement of my cock, I had never been more connected to another person. And it was then, right then, that I knew there could never be anyone else, not ever.

My heart would stop with him.

"Fuck," I grumbled, irritated that in the middle of fucking my heart had shown up. Damn inconvenient to have epiphanies while screwing.

His laughter was a surprise.

"Ef?"

"Stop thinking, because I need you here, participating," he said, chuckling. "Just hold me. Now!"

The last demand shouted brought me back to my body that I'd been checked out of for precious seconds.

Lifting him to his hands and knees, I took rough hold of his hair, bowed his back, and kept him there as I pistoned inside of him.

"Oh thank God," he rasped, his voice a hoarse whine as I drew back, dragging myself slowly over the spot that made him clench and buck, feeling every sensation he did before I pushed back in, harder and faster with each stroke.

It was the friction that did it, that made him come, but also, it was me—taking care of him, being his safety net, the man he could voice his desires to, all of them, uninhibited and vulnerable—that sent him hurtling over the edge.

He clenched around me, bearing down, his body rigid beneath mine as I followed his orgasm with my own, collapsing over him, my body draped over his.

Slowly, he sank to the blanket with me still buried inside of him, and we lay there, panting, covered in sweat, breathing in tandem.

Eventually I turned my head and kissed his sweaty temple.

"Where did you go?" he murmured, not needing me to move, instead the deep sigh of contentment letting me know he was more than happy to have me right where I was.

"I realized something."

"Tell me."

"I love you," I said honestly, my voice only hitching a bit with the emotion welling up in my chest.

A shiver ran through him from head to toe. "I love you back," he husked, and it was easy to hear the sincerity, the honesty, and understand that his heart was there for the taking.

Two days later, I knew that because I loved him, I had to change what he called me.

"Hey," Efrem said softly, standing to walk over to me, reaching out to put his hand on my cheek as soon as he could. "T? What's—"

"My name's not Terrence Moss," I told him. "It's Darius Hawthorne."

His gaze was riveted on me.

"I'm actually related to Nathaniel Hawthorne, the writer."

"I don't—"

"Do you know originally it was Hathorn?"

"I—what?"

"He added a *w* and an *e* to it."

"I have no—"

"My father told me that it was because Nathaniel didn't want people knowing he was related to the guy who was involved in the Salem Witch Trials since Hathorn was like the only one of the judges who never publicly apologized."

He was processing, eyes blinking, watching me.

"It's true, you can look it up."

"No, I believe you."

"Interesting, right?"

"I think you're missing what's truly the most riveting part of this conversation."

"My father used to tell me that he always wanted to move back to Boston. He said that some kind of genetic memory was at work."

"Terrence—*Darius*, I—"

I sighed. "I miss my father. He was funny. You would have liked him."

"I have no doubt. Anyone related to you would be amazing, I'm sure."

"My father used to have a framed print of our family crest in his study," I said absently. "I wonder if I can find one."

"Explain it from the beginning," he prodded, taking my hand and leading me over to the chaise he'd just gotten up from.

Once we were seated, facing each other, with his thumb sliding over my knuckles, he listened about my parents and how I had been Darius and how I was now Terrence.

"So nobody knows that name."

"No."

His eyes glittered in the dwindling light of the sunset as he stared at me, looking utterly besotted. I would never forget his face at that moment. "You trust me."

"More than anything or anyone," I promised him, because it was true. I had never even considered telling another soul my real name, not then, not for years after.

And then he lunged, and I went down under him, kissed hungrily, possessively, all the time with the litany of my new name—my birth name, the one I shared with him first.

Now, in the present, wanting to hear his answer, I asked Efrem again, "Do you remember when I told you? Or doesn't that matter to you anymore?"

Like old times, he searched my face, looking for something to hold on to, the person he knew even with all the years between us.

"I still see you," I assured him. "How about you? What do you see?"

"Are you baiting me? Testing me?"

"No," I said honestly, "I'd really like to know."

He deflated, and I saw the resignation on his face as he grabbed the chair he was supposed to be sitting in, dragged it around the table—making that horrible fingernails on chalkboard noise as the rough edge of the metal scraped over the concrete—and took a seat right next to me before leaning in. He put a hand on my leg to brace himself—like no time had passed—and spoke so that his warm breath grazed my ear. "I want to talk to you."

I hoped that wasn't all he wanted, because having him close to me… all I wanted to do was taste him.

"Please don't just disappear on me," he whispered urgently.

But was it a good idea to let him in? Especially at the moment, when Eastman more than likely was gunning for me and my life was changing so dramatically?

"Give me a number."

I could barely breathe, and that in and of itself scared me to death. Nothing and no one ever rattled me or pushed me off my game, ever… until right now. "It's dangerous," I whispered, my voice deserting me just when I needed it.

I knew it would be. I'd known all along, from the word go, that being anywhere near Efrem would mess with my focus and my resolve, would make me vulnerable, and in return would place him in harm's way. I'd been sure of it sixteen years ago and was sure of it now. I was pleased with myself for the choices I'd made.

"Why's that?" he asked, staring at my mouth.

It didn't make sitting in the same room with him any easier, though. We'd been apart for a bit more than a decade and a half because the brass saw in me a man they could mold into a killer with a cold, calculating brain, not a mindless brute. Had I shown less aptitude for dealing out death and more in diplomacy, I might have had something similar to Efrem's perfectly respectable career path and not my infamous one complete with medals and commendations and utter secrecy.

"Darius."

I cleared my throat. "I'm dangerous."

"You're not that scary, I assure you."

"You have no idea who I am anymore."

"Oh no?"

"No."

"I—"

"When I walk out of here, you should just forget you saw me," I said sharply, because otherwise I would have choked on the words I didn't want to say.

He scoffed. "Are you kidding? You're not walking out of here."

"I am, actually, because, like I said, I have a guy coming."

He leaned back, studying me, those brilliant emerald green eyes of his locked on my face. "But I thought—I was told you worked for yourself."

Oh....

I shifted in my seat, making myself as comfortable as I could in the hard metal chair. "What file did you get?"

"What do you mean? There's more than one?"

"Of course. I thought you were in the loop."

I remembered his glare so well that I floundered. Anything I ever did that he didn't like—or wasn't sure of—I'd been on the receiving end of the furrowed brows and flash of green. "Oh, I am most definitely in the loop. This is the Office of Homeland Security you're fucking around with."

"I'm not fucking around with anything," I said with a grin. "I'm just surprised that with whatever your clearance is, that the agency didn't send over my military file."

"I—how long did you stay with the military? Because after you were taken and I was transferred to—"

"A while," I said, not wanting to delve into the last night I saw him, but I couldn't stop the memory from flashing through my mind. We'd been caught, me and Efrem, in his little house off base because, unbeknownst to me, Efrem's buddy had been compromised and was reporting to our base commander. It had been 2001, and things were different in the military then, but some things were still the same. Consenting relationships were one thing, but officers mixing with enlisted still happened on thin ice, behind closed doors, under a constant threat of discovery. Colonel Brent Davidson authorized that we be taught a lesson about fraternization, but as things go sometimes, you get enough men together and the mob mentality takes over.

Efrem was making chicken carbonara. I was sitting on the counter drinking a bottle of water and watching him when the front door of the tiny A-frame was kicked open and we had soldiers, men he knew because he roared at them by name, in the living room.

"The hell are you doing?" Efrem yelled, charging toward them, sure that it was a mistake, certain that he could disperse them with only his voice.

But there were seven of them, and they surged around him, two guys grabbing his arms while the third punched him squarely in the face. He would have fallen if they weren't holding him up.

"You like dick, huh, Lahm?" the leader, Leonard Barnes, Efrem had called him, catcalled as the other four men cornered me in the small kitchen.

"Get the fuck out of my house!" Efrem roared again, his gaze flicking to me, checking, more frightened for me than himself.

"I know you like that big black dick on Moss over there," he snickered, working open his belt, "but you're just gonna have to make do."

"You stay right there, boy," one of the men closest to me scoffed, "maybe you'll learn a little something."

"I say he gets fucked too," another guy crowed.

"Nah," the guy on my left said darkly. "I think a good old-fashioned lynching is the only way to go."

Efrem screamed at that and kept shrieking until Barnes punched him in the gut, stilling his cry of terror.

I saw Barnes yank Efrem's pants and briefs down and bare his ass before he slapped it, and the thought hit me that these men had made their intentions known, and the others, by their silence, had agreed. Not one of them had spoken up, said they should stop, think; it was only them egging each other on, and my focus tunneled down to Efrem—to reaching Efrem. I would not let them defile him. I would do whatever was in my power to prevent that.

Thinking back on that moment, as I had many times in my life, I always wondered at their stupidity. And yes, they didn't know me, had no idea about the training I'd received and had no clue how easily I'd taken to it, but more than that, they'd cornered me in the kitchen.

Stupid. And careless. Mostly stupid.

I grabbed the chef's knife Efrem had been using from the cutting board and drove it into the throat of the guy on my right. The blood from his severed carotid momentarily blinded the guy beside him, so

I went low and put the knife first into his gut, then pulled it out and drove it hard into his sternum.

I left it there as the next two guys rushed me, and I grabbed the pot of boiling water off the stove and flung it at them. They were screaming as I grabbed the frying pan full of crackling oil for the chicken and threw that as well.

As the rapist and the guy who wanted to hang me stood there, hands on their faces, crying, I grabbed lynching guy's gun and shot them both in the head, one after the other, right through their fingers.

"Holy fuck!" Barnes screamed as I came forward just as I'd been taught, both hands on the weapon, arms tight but not locked, shooting the first guy who lifted his hands in surrender as he let go of Efrem and then the second as he scuttled backward against the wall.

Efrem scrambled to his feet, yanking up his pants, and I checked him, once, making sure he was okay before I turned my attention to Barnes.

"Jesus Christ, Moss, we were only gonna scare you."

"Shouldn't kid," I said flatly, hearing the first siren in the distance.

It was fast once I had the gun, the pop-pop-pop as I did my killing, and as big as the man's eyes were, how wide, I understood that he was utterly shell-shocked.

Barnes sagged to his knees, hands laced on top of his head. He must not have even considered reaching for his gun that Efrem, using a tissue from the box on the end table, took off of him.

Efrem walked over to the cut-out ledge near the kitchen, and his gaze met mine. "I couldn't—did they hurt you?"

"No," I huffed, trying to catch my breath, unable to, the pounding in my ears hard to hear around as well.

When he moved over to me, into my space so I could put an arm around him, hold him solidly against me and keep the gun trained on Barnes, finally, only then, could I breathe.

The police were there moments later, and Efrem and I were facedown on his carpet as Barnes babbled about scaring us and how I'd gone nuts and attacked him and his guys.

Outside in the hot, sticky sweltering summer air of Savannah, Efrem and I were separated into different police cruisers, and through the window, staring at him, his scared eyes on me, was the last time I saw him for nearly two decades.

Many hours later, I was surprised when a man I'd never seen before walked into the room as I sat in the brig at Hunter.

He was tall, broad shouldered, and from the way the shirt clung, muscular. It wasn't his physique that made me stare, though; it was his eyes and the expression in them. The midnight blue color soaked up the light, and the way he was scrutinizing me, like he was deciding something, put me on edge.

"Sergeant Terrence Moss?"

"Yes," I answered, not standing because I saw no uniform.

He moved to the bars and crossed his arms. "You're going to be tried for the murder of six men, Moss."

"It was self-defense," I said flatly, not leaping to my feet, not charging the bars, my training ingrained. Emotions had no place in interrogations. Remain calm, centered, keep your voice level and noncombative. The first person who cracked, lost.

"Says you."

"What does Barnes say?"

He tipped his head sideways. "That doesn't matter."

"Why not?"

"He's an unreliable witness."

"And why is that?"

"In his version, they were just there to put the fear of God into you for being faggots."

I watched his eyes as he used that repellant word and noted his own lack of emotion. "So everyone is buying that story?"

"I didn't say that."

"Where's Efrem?"

"The question isn't where he *is*, but where he's *going*, and that is all dependent on you."

"Me," I said flatly, a statement, not a question.

He nodded slowly.

I studied him, the long sleek lines of him, the handsome face with features carved out of granite, but with the eyes of a predator. "What is this? Who are you?"

Uncrossing his arms, he reached through the bars to shake my hand, and the smile I got was real, creased laugh lines, genuinely warm. "I'm Dante Cerreto, and I'm here to make you an offer you shouldn't refuse."

Hard to say what got me off the hard metal shelf of a seat and across the cell to him but some of it had to be the grin. He'd amused himself, that was clear, and that in turn allowed me to breathe for what felt like the first time in hours. His hand was warm and dry, the shake firm, and then he nodded, jaw clenched, hoarsely telling me that everything was going to be all right. It was like he knew what it was like to be where I was, on the other side of the bars.

I was given a choice: be tried and court-martialed, then transferred to Leavenworth to await execution by lethal injection, or… door number two. I could leave immediately and serve my country in an altogether different capacity.

"And what would that be?"

I listened as he outlined the job in that quick-and-dirty way military men had, told me the worst and got it out of the way, no beating around the bush, instead cutting to the heart of the matter.

"You want me to train to be an assassin?" I summarized when he was done, still unsure that I'd heard him right, as farfetched as it sounded.

"You killed six people in *seconds*, Moss, and as far as I can tell from what Barnes and your boyfriend said, you didn't even break a sweat."

"No, that's—"

"Do you feel any remorse?" he asked, his voice low, husky, the sound soothing at the moment as my life unraveled.

I glared at him. "Why would I feel any remorse? They came to rape Efrem and kill me."

"As I said before, Barnes says no, that he was tasked with scaring you by Davidson, nothing else."

"And what, he just gets away with what he did?"

"No one is getting away with anything, I assure you."

"What about Davidson?"

"He's done" were his simple words, and I could tell he meant it.

"But if you know that I'm innocent then—"

"You're not innocent," he objected. "You didn't need to kill the men who had Lieutenant Lahm. They were both giving up."

"You kill them so they can't come back and get you later."

"Agreed," Cerreto said with a nod. "You eliminate all threats, that's what we're taught. But that's not what this was."

"The hell it wasn't."

"No," he said implacably. "They threatened the man you love, so you put them down."

"They broke into the house!" I yelled. "Take me to court, I know that—"

"You're a soldier," he reminded me. "There won't be any civilian court for you."

"I refuse to believe that—"

"This isn't *a movie*, sergeant," he reminded me. "That's not how this works."

I stared into all the dark, inky blue made almost black under the fluorescent lights.

"You will be tried by possibly homophobic white middle-aged men who will not like the idea of a black man getting away with what you're charged with."

He was right, of course, but I was not ready to concede.

"If you agree to come with me, Efrem Lahm will be safe with a clean record and no mention of this incident."

"You're telling me that you're going to trade his future for mine?"

"I'm telling you that *you* could keep his record spotless."

"Because, what, he's worth more because he's white?"

He squinted at me like I was nuts, that I'd somehow disappointed him with my assessment. "I don't give a shit about him, Moss. He could be anyone, any race, any color, any creed. He could be a she for all I care, your partner is only important as leverage because *you* love him, that's all."

I absorbed that.

"He's important if he gives you to us and meaningless the second after that," he explained. "What we do isn't about anything but the best, and because my boss has had his eye on you, I'm here making you a once-in-a-lifetime offer. But never for a second believe that he is more valuable than you because it's very clearly the reverse."

I took a breath. "Assassins, trained killers. You're talking about black ops."

"Yes."

"You're talking about the CIA."

"I am. Yes."

"Would I still be in the Army?"

"Yes."

"What's the difference?"

"New name, new everything, and you never see Efrem Lahm again, because if you agree, you die right here, right now."

I concentrated on keeping my breathing even. "You work for the agency?"

"I do."

"You're out of the military now?"

"For quite some time, yes."

I studied his face. "Have you killed a lot of people, Cerreto?"

"Yes, I have, but I'm about ready to cut ties myself. It's time for a family for me. I already have the guy, just waiting to see if we got the kid."

The words, so matter-of-factly spoken, floored me. "They—the agency—they don't care about the gay thing?"

"They don't ask, as you know."

I swallowed hard. "I want it in writing that Efrem will be safe."

"Of course."

"Am I allowed to say goodbye?"

"No," he replied quickly, and I could hear the catch in his voice like maybe that was hard for him to say. "Once you say yes to me, Lahm is on the next plane to California."

"He'll just come right back here; he'll never stop looking for me."

"He won't have a choice."

I understood. This was the military, the government, after all. When they wanted you gone, as well as all trace of you, they could make that happen.

"Darius!" Efrem broke into my memories, and I was faced with his ragged gaze. He was caught somewhere between anger and sadness.

"What do you want me to tell you?"

"Everything!" he yelled. "One minute you were there, in my life, the next you were gone."

"How else did you see that playing out?" I asked gently.

"I could have been discharged," he rasped. "We both could have."

"And then what? What would that have served?"

His eyes narrowed. "You made a deal."

It was so easy for me to lie. My career—my *life*—was based on being able to talk or shoot my way out of danger. But Efrem was different. The one lie I'd ever told him—my name—I had come clean on. Just looking at him made me want to start from when I'd last seen him and bring him up to speed on everything I'd ever done. My past was, at the least, disconcerting; at the most, horrifying. My biggest concern, though, was that our time was ticking down. I didn't want to leave him. I didn't want to go.

"Darius!" he barked. "Tell me!"

I coughed, shifting around in my seat. "What is it that you want to know about Eastman?"

"Eastman," he repeated, like the name was something in his mouth he wanted to spit out. "I want to know about you!"

"But legally you're holding me about Eastman, right?"

"I'm holding you for whatever reason I deem fit."

"Are we being recorded?" I had to ask.

"No, we're not being recorded. Now answer the goddamn question!"

"Legally you're required to be recording this," I reminded him.

"Oh, am I?" he asked snidely.

I'd been in my share of nonrecorded interviews that ended in torture, and since I was confident that wasn't about to happen, a flicker of worry—for him—seeped into me.

"You should turn on the recording," I apprised him. "You don't want to do anything to jeopardize your standing with—"

"Tell me where you've been," he demanded under his breath, from the way he was huffing, barely holding it together.

"This is not the time or place for—"

"Oh, I think it is," he snarled, indicating the cuffs on my wrists with a tip of his head. "You're not going anywhere until I get my answers."

But I was, and too soon at that. I wanted to talk to him just as much as he wanted me to, but I couldn't, and that was the truth.

"Tell me what happened that night," he insisted, his voice cracking with the strain. "I need to know!"

"It's not—"

"If you say it's not important, I'll shoot you right here."

I couldn't help the grin; it came too fast. The very idea that Efrem Lahm would ever hurt me on purpose was laughable. Preposterous.

"Don't you dare laugh!"

"Shoot me?" I repeated his words, squinting at him. "Really?"

"I want answers."

I shook my head. The separation had been painful enough. I didn't need to talk about what had really happened, where I'd gone to get ready for a new phase in my life.

He took a breath. "You owe me an explanation."

"Not me," I corrected. "I could tell you, but I'm not the one who separated us."

"Don't you think I know that?" he said, his voice thready and sharp. I could hear the pain in it clear as day. "I just want to know why."

Some pieces I could tell because I didn't work for the agency anymore. There would never be repercussions because no one could prove a thing. "I had a choice."

"To save me."

"There's more to it than that."

"I'm sure there is, but why did you get a choice in the first place?"

"You know why."

He shook his head. "I don't."

"You do if you think about it a second."

"You weren't—we weren't on anybody's radar." I stared at him until he threw up his hands in defeat. "Fine, I knew they were watching you. I would have had to be blind to miss it."

"It wasn't overt," I granted, "but with my training, what they were having me do, it made sense. I just didn't know the signs then, didn't know what to look out for. That night, what happened, that was all they needed to get all the way interested in recruiting me."

He considered that, scowling, searching his memory, I was certain, piecing through the details of that night. "You mean how you did it, not what you did," he said, not saying the actual words: how fast I'd killed six men.

"Yes."

"I don't—"

"Yes, you do."

"You're saying that the—"

"They wanted me," I said, stopping him from saying the agency or the company or coming right out and saying CIA. He'd been safe a long time; I didn't need him jeopardizing anything this late in the game.

"I know that," he whispered. "How could I not?"

He was a very smart man, keen judge of character, of happenings, of the why and the ins and outs. Of course he'd seen the agenda for what it was.

"The base commander had us watched. Torian, my friend, who I trusted—" He choked on the words. "He told them when we'd be together, and so they caught us there, that night, on purpose, and after everything, they got to take you away."

"There was only one choice to be made, and I made it," I confessed.

"You gave up your freedom and our plans to keep me safe."

I lifted my head. "With how things happened, there was no happy ending there, no 'everyone walks.' It wasn't going to go that way."

"Yes, but I could have gone with you."

"No, no, you had your whole life to—"

"My life was you!"

I couldn't look at him, so I concentrated on the table instead, and the cuffs, realizing how easily I could get out of them if I wanted.

"Darius!"

My head snapped up, and my gaze hit his, crashed into all the gorgeous rich color. "They didn't want you," I explained hesitantly. "The deal on the table was to leave you alone, not take you as well."

"Which makes sense," he admitted, biting his bottom lip before he went on. "I was never good at split-second decisions, not like you, and I knew what was happening with your training, I'm not stupid. The upper brass, they always wanted you. Everyone noticed, everyone saw."

They had, it was stupid to deny. I excelled in areas that kept me on their radar: closequarters training, shooting, hunting, hiding, and most of all, last-minute tactical maneuvers where I left my team to complete a mission. The objective was the most important outcome, and I knew when to detach from my team, to send them on while I remained behind.

"I knew your CO wanted you to step up to black ops, to take a different path from being a soldier to being an assassin."

"You make it sound so cool," I said wistfully, wishing it had been so dramatic or heroic or anything but the chilling display of indifference that it had been. No one cared about the individual, only the objective, only the bigger picture. There was no concern for a singular cog in the machine. "But it doesn't matter how I served, just that I did."

"Of course it matters," he hissed, eyes narrowed, muscles in his jaw working. "One way, the way we planned, saw us out in four years and together and the other way... how things happened... that broke us apart."

I gestured at him. "But it turned out all right. You've done well."

He scoffed, almost a choke. "I was a mediocre soldier, and I've been a mediocre agent," he conceded. "There was nothing ever remotely amazing about me."

"That's categorically untrue," I stated, daring him to argue with me. "You're amazing."

His eyes filled fast, and he wiped at them roughly, taking a breath, trying to settle himself. "No, that's you, always were perfect in every way."

"You're deluded and—"

"It was easy to see. You were so bright, like a beacon, and that's why they saw you. No way to miss you."

I shook my head slowly, swallowing before I spoke, but still my voice came out crackly. "I would never have traded—"

"Your life, your plans, your freedom—"

"Shut up," I ordered him. "It wasn't like that."

"It was exactly that, and we both know it." Efrem took a shuddering breath. "They wanted you, and because of me, because I trusted my friend even though you said not to, because of Davidson we—"

"They pressured him," I defended. Torian Black, his friend, was a guy who would have never thought twice about laying himself over a tripwire for Efrem. "I found that out later. It wasn't his fault. You need to let that go."

"Oh?"

"His wife was Iraqi, right? You remember that."

He jolted and was suddenly staring at me, mouth open, stunned.

"He's fine, so is she. They live in Paris, and they have three kids. But don't think for a second that he didn't have a dog in that fight too."

"I forgot about—I—"

"He did what he had to, I did what I had to. Your part was only to live your life."

"So you think, what, I had it easy?"

"That's not what I'm saying. What I'm saying is that we all had to deal with the fallout from that night, and we all made choices based on what we could live with."

"Not all of us," he retorted. "I had no choice. Because if I had, it certainly would not have been to lose my best friend and the love of my life."

I'd been stabbed many times over the course of my career, but that jab hurt more than any one of them.

"And I don't mean Torian when I say best friend. I mean you on both counts."

I knew that, I didn't need him to tell me.

"I have not missed one day without a thought of you in all this time."

Neither had I. "Not just you," I murmured.

We sat there, staring, neither moving.

"I missed your eyes," he mused, taking a breath. "I've never met anyone else with spring green eyes with gold in them."

I had so much to say, but our time was getting shorter, I was certain of it. "Efrem—"

"Explain things to me like I haven't seen you in sixteen years, ten months, nine hours, and three minutes."

But who was counting. "I'm not a contract killer," I responded.

"Oh yes you—"

"I mean," I offered, putting one cuffed hand on the top of the file—my file—he'd obviously been reading from and moving it from one side of the table to where he now sat. "I was up until very recently, but I'm not now."

"What the hell does that mean?"

I grimaced.

"Tell me," he demanded, balling his hands into fists so ostensibly I couldn't see them shake, staring at me like he was trying to memorize my face.

"Ef, I—"

"I want to know everything that happened to you since I saw you last."

My chuckle was soft. "That would take days."

"We've got time for you to start."

"Hardly," I replied, hearing the sadness in my voice. I wanted to stay there and sit with him for no earthly reason other than pure selfishness. I used to miss him so much that my bones ached with it, but that had finally dissipated a bit over time. Seeing him now was like a punch in the gut. But still, he couldn't be a part of my life, and that revelation was painful. He was with Homeland, and I was on the other side. He could never be with me and retain his career or his life as he knew it. Being with me would change everything, and I wasn't stupid. I knew the difference between reality and fairy tales. It wasn't possible, so opening up to him was a waste of time.

He tilted forward. "I don't think you understand the precarious position you're in. We have you and your partner on—"

"He's a friend."

"Pardon me?"

"Trevan Bean," I clarified. "He's a friend, nothing more, and I was there to watch his back and make sure no one tried to kill him."

"And I care that the world would be free of one more gun-smuggling—"

"He's not moving guns," I stated, almost letting it slip that Trevan had already dismantled that operation. But being reformed would still get him thrown into prison for the rest of his natural life. "He's not doing anything you think he is, and when I walk out of here, he's coming with me."

"Oh, baby, we're the government."

I smiled, and he jerked like an electrical current zipped through him, realizing, I was certain, from the stricken look on his face, what he'd said.

"Jesus." His voice was gruff with emotion, and he had to put his hand on the table, seemingly for balance. "I... where did—"

"Yep," I teased. "'Baby' just came right back."

We were both floundering, absolutely unable to restore professional decorum even for a second. Normally I would never allow a moment where I let my defenses down, but this was Efrem I was talking to, and my memories of him drowned all my logic. My gut reaction was to simply unload the truth on him.

He was in exactly the same boat, and I could tell from his rough breathing, the furrow of his brows, the pain in his gaze, but mostly in the way he kept leaning toward me and catching himself. Clearly, he was fighting the urge to lunge at me.

"I—"

"I promise you, he's not trafficking guns."

"Oh, no, of course he isn't," he placated me. It was a tone I'd never heard from him before and one I didn't like. Jaded did not fit well on my ex.

I put my manacled hand on his wrist and gently squeezed my fingertips on the pulse point there. "He's not."

"You're telling me that he's not moving guns, but if he's not, then why was he leaving Eastman's home to begin with?"

Implicating Trevan, for any reason, even to save him, was not something I was prepared to do. "He was saying goodbye."

"And I'm just supposed to take your word that he's not in the gun business anymore?"

"No. You can check. You can talk to anyone, and they'll tell you that he used to move products—manure, mulch, sod—and moved on to things like dog food and then went into renting out his warehouse space and finally sold them."

"That's not possible."

"It might have looked like gun trafficking on the outside, but I can assure you that no one in Detroit has ever bought guns from Trevan Bean."

"So you're telling me that he's the only legitimate part of Thiago Fanton's business in Detroit?"

"Yes."

"And you expect me to buy that?"

"No, like I said, you can look into it and verify everything I just told you."

He stared at me, and as I gazed back, I noted, as I always had, how gorgeous his eyes were. The green was really just beautiful. Like lying on my side in the grass in the deep shade, the green so dark it held traces of midnight blue at the tips that I could see catching faint traces of dappled light.

I could still remember reporting to my CO's office that morning to meet the new twenty-two-year-old second lieutenant transferred into our company after our last one froze in the middle of a street, too scared to go forward and too terrified to retreat. He'd died there, and I'd nearly died retrieving him, but he'd always talked about his mother, and I wasn't about to let her not have him to bury. I'd been a newly promoted staff sergeant then, all of twenty-four, thinking I knew everything, there with three others, not looking forward to meeting the new guy, wondering how long this one would last and what college he was from. But when my gaze locked on the man standing beside the desk, I found the air had gone thin as I tried to catch my breath.

His gaze didn't waver. There was strength to it, and power. The other guys had been hopeful; I was enthralled. I just wanted to talk to him. Of course, with us being separated by rank and privilege, I was sure I never had a chance, but it turned out that when he looked up and saw me, he saw someone he wanted as well. But that was much later, us talking during lazy Sundays spent in bed. In that moment there was only me being dismissed along with the others.

At dusk, I was walking toward the barracks, and when my name was called, I'd turned and he was there, the new lieutenant. I came sharply to attention and was floored when he walked right up to me, too close, head tipped, staring into my eyes.

"At ease, sergeant," he whispered, inhaling deeply.

As alluring as I found him, no one, ever, had any power over me besides rank for a legitimate reason. His interest, communicated by his baited breath and how he stared into my eyes, had nothing but physical attraction marking it. I'd wanted him from the second I saw him as well, but for it to work, there could never be a question that we were equals. I wouldn't have it any other way.

"Permission to speak freely," I growled, excited and irritated at the same time.

"At ease," he replied hoarsely, lips parted, eyes on mine, zeroed in there.

"This is bullshit," I bit off the words. "You don't get to do this to me."

"Do what to you?"

"Stop me with your rank on a whim."

He seemed startled and took a step back. "I—no, I didn't mean—"

I went back to attention. "Permission to leave, sir?"

He stammered out his agreement, and I turned on my heel and left.

A week later, at a local dive bar down on Abercorn, I was shooting pool with other guys from my unit when Efrem came in with Torian Black and some other friends. I'd been ducking him since our first encounter, walking out of rooms he walked into, seeing him only when we were training or sitting in briefings. When he came to the table, the rest of his guys in tow, and asked if we wanted to play, my buddy Jake Sawyer voiced concern: if we wiped the floor with the officers on a Friday night, what would Monday morning look like?

"We're assholes," Torian assured him, "but we're not total pricks."

Everyone laughed, and that was it, tension broken.

When I went to get a round of drinks, Efrem quickly volunteered to go with me. As we stood at the bar waiting, me facing the bartender, him at my shoulder, I felt him lean close, just a brush of contact that could have been incidental, but the inhale a second later, close to my ear, was on purpose. Or not.

It might have been that he couldn't help himself. That thought did warm things to my stomach and cock.

I turned my head to look at him and realized that his eyes were everywhere but meeting mine. I wasn't just being checked out, I was being cataloged. "Hey."

His head snapped up and the guilty look on his face was obvious and adorable. "What?" He almost gasped, startled as he was.

"Did you just smell me?"

"I—what?"

I scowled at him so I wouldn't smile. This beautiful man who couldn't lie at all, who was very clearly into me, there was no way not to be interested right back. But I had to make a decision because I needed a balance of power. So now, if I wanted anything more from him, then I would have to be the one to initiate. It was easy to see I made him more than a little nervous, for probably more than one reason. Attraction was one thing, being unsure where you stood another, but the military aspect on top of it made our interaction... precarious. We each had to be sure of the other, and that would be difficult unless someone bit the bullet and came out and asked. Since maybe that had been what he was trying to do the day he attempted to talk to me, I figured it was my turn to take a breath and dive in.

After we returned with the round of beers, I moved over to the back wall and leaned, waiting to see what he would do. It took only seconds and he was there, beside me, close, ostensibly waiting for his turn to play, brushing his shoulder with mine.

"That day you came up to talk to me," I said without turning to look at him, "did you have something you wanted?"

"Yes," he replied gruffly.

I crossed my arms before glancing over at him. "What was that?"

"Are you—I mean, I wasn't sure if you were interested in what I had to say."

"I am," I assured him.

"I never meant to make you feel uncomfortable."

I nodded. "It could be that I have authority issues."

Tentative smile then, just a trace curling his lush mouth. "I could have handled things better, but I was a bit overwhelmed."

Nice to hear. "Oh?"

"Yes," he whispered.

"So, then we've come to a new understanding, don't you think?"

"Please… yes, good." The words tumbled out of him nonsensically. "We have."

"You're sure?"

Those gorgeous emerald eyes of his, glittering in the neon lights of the bar, were huge as he stared at me and nodded slowly.

"You want to do things with me?"

"I do—yes. Whatever you like."

"Okay, then, I usually get a room over at the Econo Lodge down the street so when I pick somebody up, I can just take them there."

I heard him catch his breath.

"If I asked you to come with me, would—"

"Yes," he blurted.

"Did you all ride together?"

"We took a cab," he explained, shifting closer to me, bumping my arm with his. "I can leave now and—"

"We can walk there," I told him. "Just meet me around back in fifteen minutes."

I pushed off the wall then, put up my cue, walked over to Jake and leaned in. I told him I was leaving to get laid and went out the back.

Standing under a tree in the shadows behind what could loosely be described as a dirt and gravel parking lot, I waited only ten minutes before Efrem was there, opening and closing the door behind him, scanning the area for me.

I whistled for him, and he jogged over, ducking under a low-hanging branch to join me in the darkness.

"Your buddy, does he know you're gay?"

"Yeah, why?"

He cleared his throat. "The way he told it, you were going on a booty call with some girl."

"Well, yeah, this is the Army, right?"

"Sure," he agreed, staring, moving closer, crowding me.

"Are you gay, bi, straight but wanting to——"

"Gay," he said quickly, swallowing hard. "Just like you."

We were quiet, each waiting, surveying the other.

I said what I assumed he was thinking as well. "This could have been a trap."

"I thought of that," he confessed, his hand slipping to my hip, one of his fingers catching in my belt loop. "But I decided I was going with hope instead of being chickenshit about everything like I usually am."

"Are you?"

He nodded as his other hand, his right, pressed over my heart. "I don't... I've never been interested in another soldier before, and so usually I'll see someone when I'm out and it's easy enough not to act on that feeling, that excitement. The moment passes and it's a missed opportunity, yes, but I'm still safe. I haven't risked anything."

"I get that."

"But that day in the office—I nearly swallowed my tongue."

I smiled at him. The honesty was refreshing.

"And I thought: I'm going to be around this man, and I thought: maybe he's looking at me back, and it's definitely lust at first sight because I can't get him out of my mind."

"I felt the same," I admitted. This was about us being on equal footing. It was important. The balance of us having identical thought processes put things in perspective.

"Then why were you upset that day? And why did you work so hard at putting space between us?"

"To make sure we were both serious."

"Well, I am," he told me. "Serious."

I nodded.

"So are we going or——"

"We've got to check first and make sure we're compatible," I said as I leaned in.

I was a player before Efrem Lahm kissed me. I was the one who initiated, I was the one who fucked and forgot, who barely got first names and was never interested enough to ask for or give out a number. But that changed when he met me halfway, wrapped his arms around my neck, making sure I couldn't get away, and kissed me hard and deep and with so much frustrated need I felt it roll through me like I was being tumbled by a wave, left disoriented but not hurt, not drowned. It was just a wake-up call that the ocean had all the power. And in that moment, I understood that whatever equal footing I thought I had with him was a delusion. Because when you wanted to be with someone, when another person had all your attention, that took you out at the knees and left you floundering.

I clutched at him, crushing him against me, and he whined into my mouth, grinding his groin into mine, pushing, trying to wedge in closer.

One of my hands moved to his ass, and when I squeezed tight, he broke the kiss to let his head fall back, and moan. It was decadent and pained, and I knew that if I didn't get us out of the trees and to the motel, we were in trouble. That fast, we were ready to sate the desire burning between us.

Letting him go, I took his arm and yanked him after me until we hit the street.

"I miss your hand already," he confessed as he walked along beside me.

"Well, I don't want us to get shot out here," I said, quickening my pace. "Because gay and interracial, I think we're pushing it."

"Absolutely," he agreed, putting his hand on my shoulder, slowing me. "But this is okay. This is just two guys walking together."

I turned to look at him, wondering why we both weren't running to get to the motel when he smiled at me, and I nearly stumbled. His ease, like we had all the time in the world, like we were just out for a stroll, was somehow comforting.

"Are we not in a hurry?"

"Why? I'm not going anywhere. Are you?"

I wasn't, no.

"It's a nice night, not too hot yet, the breeze is cool, and it smells like it's going to rain."

Slowing, enjoying the sound of his voice, I took a breath.

"It smells like grass and jasmine out here."

"Yes, it does." I sighed.

"I plan on more than just this one night," he whispered.

Those kinds of words usually scared me to death. "You don't think that's a bit too optimistic?"

"I don't."

"Why not?"

"I have a feeling," he sighed, staring at me.

"It's not going to be easy."

"Anything worth doing seldom is."

I was surprised when we got to the motel, and instead of clawing at each other, we sank to the bed holding hands.

"Tell me something nobody else knows," he prodded.

When my gaze met his, I realized he was serious, and even more surprising was that I *wanted* to talk to him. It was a stunning development. Who knew talking could be so hot?

We ended up telling each other anything that came into our heads until right before dawn, and then we fell asleep, him draped over me like a blanket. I couldn't remember having ever slept more soundly. The steady beat of his heart was like coming home.

The next night, when I brought a bag over to his sweet little 750-square-foot A-frame, he launched himself at me as soon as the door closed.

After he kissed me breathless, as I held him in my arms, my hands supporting his ass as his long legs wrapped tightly around my hips, I smiled wide.

"I'm liking this welcome," I confessed, feeling a clenching inside, like I was trying to hold myself together. My reaction to him was scary, immediate and overwhelming. Being with him was too much and not enough at the same time. I'd been alone so long, and I was careful about not letting people in, and out of nowhere was *this man* and I felt like I was unraveling so fast, too fast, after only one night together, and that didn't seem smart.

"I'm liking you in my home," he murmured before mauling my mouth, grinding against me.

My head told me I was being reckless because, clearly, this man already had a hold on me that was dangerous. Hearts were lost to men like him.

"You should stay here," he said between urgent kisses. "Stay in my house, with me. I'll keep you safe. I'll take care of you."

I deepened the kiss, held him still as I sucked on his tongue and showed him slow and steady and then frantic up until I had to pull free for air.

"Oh, you're going to be mine," he whispered against the skin on my throat as he tried to get his breathing under control.

I shivered. It sounded like a promise, his words, and finding myself ready and willing was a brand new experience.

Once I put him on his feet, he led me down the hall to his bedroom to show me where to drop my duffel.

"You could have just directed me," I assured him, grinning as I followed.

"Uh-huh," he agreed, taking the bag out of my hand and dropping it beside the door before turning me around and shoving me backward.

Because I wasn't ready for it, all the abrupt movement, I got tripped up and toppled onto the bed. Before I could climb off, he pounced on me, straddling my thighs.

"I thought you cooked," I teased.

"It's in the oven," he said, curling forward, pinning my wrists to the bed and staring down at me. "I made baked parmesan crusted chicken; it's got some time left."

"Does it?" I asked, because between the gorgeous man on top of me and the smell coming from the kitchen, I was pretty certain I never wanted to leave.

He practically purred, and the sound was low and sexy. I couldn't help but buck against him. His hands were tight on my wrists, and he was using his full weight to trap me under him, settling his ass over my groin.

"Enjoying yourself?" I croaked.

"Very much so, yes," he husked, sliding his crease over the thickening bulge in my jeans.

"You're playing with fire."

"Oh God, I hope so," he said, his voice dropping into a whisper, and he tightened his thighs around my hips.

"Fuck," I groaned, pushing up into him, wanting more friction, my body knowing what I instinctively needed even if my brain was working to remain logical, to not attack him and take what I wanted.

"We talked last time," he said, releasing my wrists and rolling off me, but only long enough to shuck his shorts and briefs and then scramble to make quick work of my belt buckle and the button on my jeans. "I don't want to talk anymore."

"Not ever?" I barely got out.

"Maybe tomorrow," he teased, unzipping me just enough to fish out my cock and take both his and mine in hand and press them together.

"Oh God," I groaned, shivering under him as he rubbed the precome seeping from the head of his dick over mine, the silky slide of smooth flesh utterly carnal.

"Tell me how bad you want to be inside me."

The slow, sensuous stroking made my eyes flutter shut even as I felt him shift over me for a second before he placed a tube in my hand.

"You don't mess around," I said, my eyes drifting open so I could look up at him.

"I know what I want," he told me, and I watched the flush travel in large red blotches up his throat to his face.

"So do I," I said, smiling.

His answering grin and sigh were enough to stop my heart.

"Darius," Efrem breathed, his voice easing me from the past to the present as he leaned forward over the table and my cuffed wrists. "I want to see you."

But it wasn't safe, would never be safe, and I would not start putting him in danger now after so very long. I had thought, maybe, that once I was out from under the company's thumb that I could take back the life I wanted, but in reality, that door had opened and closed years earlier. "You can't."

"Why can't I?"

I shook my head. "You don't understand."

"Then help me to understand."

The way he was looking at me, head tipped slightly down, left eyebrow lifted, waiting, was so achingly familiar that I nearly swallowed my tongue. I desperately wanted to reach for him.

"Tell me where you've been and who you've been with."

Been with?

That was oddly phrased.

Been with was something your lover asked. Who have you been with? It was an accusation, or a courtesy when they already knew. It was not the question Efrem should have been asking.

What I heard when he said *been with* was *worked with*—which put our conversation in a different arena altogether. It moved us from reunion to interrogation.

What did he really want to know?

And then something terrible, something *ugly*, occurred to me, something almost sickening, truly disheartening and altogether awful. I leaned back, squinting.

"Darius?"

"Who's asking these questions?"

"I'm sorry?"

"I mean, who wants these answers?"

"What are you asking me?"

"Do *you* want to know where I've been or does *Homeland* want to know?"

His mouth dropped open.

"Well?"

"You did not just say that to me."

He hadn't denied it. He deflected instead. "Evasion. Nice."

"No, that's not—"

"You didn't flat-out refute it."

"Because this is me!"

But really? I had no idea who he truly was, not anymore. How could I? And he didn't know me, but he knew what he wanted. He wanted answers, and more than just those about what happened to me that night so long ago. He wanted to know all about me… and Trevan.

It was his job. He'd gone there in pursuit of my friend, not me, and the only reason he wasn't in the room with Trevan was because I was possibly the bigger fish. It would have been nice to think that it was our shared ancient history, that he'd missed me as much as I'd missed him, but was that it? Because there I was, delivered to him on a platter, and what a coup it would be for him to penetrate my defenses, to break down who I was and what I'd done. His Christmas bonus would be really good this year if I would roll over and play ball with him.

It occurred to me that I was possibly being ridiculous. If the roles were reversed, I would have beaten the truth out of him. But on the other hand, I would have never let him disappear to begin with. How hard had he looked? That night in the brig with Dante Cerreto I had boasted that nothing would stop Efrem from finding me, and yet… he never had. And now here he was, with the opportunity to not only ask questions about Trevan but about me as well—and was I positive that he didn't know who I was, who I'd been? He was a Homeland Security agent. Maybe he had all my files and all I was seeing was what he wanted me to. Perhaps, I was being expertly played.

The only part I knew was completely hidden was me being the vault, but I was the vault for these exact reasons. Being paranoid, asking questions—these were things I needed to do to prevent damage, prevent exposure… prevent abandonment.

"Darius, you can't for a moment believe that—"

"Wait," I whispered, lost for a moment like I never was now and had not been since I was very young. Since my parents—

"Darius!"

I put my hand up to make him stop because I needed a second to think.

Never could I be accused of being stupid. I knew who I was, had only my own thoughts to examine in many situations I'd found myself in over the years, and so the idea that I didn't know what was going on in my own head was ludicrous.

Twice in my life people had been taken from me: once, when I lost my parents as a child, once when I made the decision to save Efrem. I finally, just recently, had begun to trust other people, and "friends" was now a warm word, not merely a euphemism for people who wouldn't shoot me on sight. When I had told Trevan years ago that I had ten friends in the world, the list consisted not of people I would spend an evening eating with, but of those whom would be my spotter or hide a gun for me. Not counting Duncan Stiel, a childhood friend I couldn't shake.

Becoming the vault changed my thinking about what I could have, who I could be. I never thought I'd live past thirty, and then when forty came and went, that had been another surprise. I was finally ready to have people in my life, hence the sharing of my real name, and what had been even crazier was thinking, just for a moment, that the door I thought was closed on Efrem could be opened again.

It was sad to realize I would never be able to trust him enough to try.

"Darius!" he yelled.

"Sorry," I said automatically.

"The only thing I care about is finding out where you've been."

Not the truth.

"Look at me."

I hadn't realized I'd glanced away until he brought my attention to the fact.

"Listen to me."

"What?" I asked coolly.

He scowled at me, and I turned away from him again.

"You're like a wall."

We were done talking.

"You know me!" he shouted. I heard the crack in his voice, and I met his gaze. "Darius. You know me."

I thought I did. Or always would. I'd run through this reunion a million times in my head. What it would look like, sound like, but me unsure of his motives had never once crossed my mind. Him playing me was a brand-new scenario.

"Do I?"

He was stunned, mouth open, eyes wide, pale, looking lost, floundering. "The hell are you saying right now?"

I nodded. "I think I'll just sit here, thanks."

"Darius, you can't think that—"

"Oh, I do think."

"How dare you question me!" He was incredulous. "You can't actually believe that I would—this is me!"

"You're good. I almost bought it," I baited him. "That you missed me."

"Darius!" he roared, and the door opened at the same time.

"Agent Lahm."

"Get out!"

"Agent Lahm." His name was repeated more firmly by the large man in an ill-fitting suit now standing in the doorway. Had Efrem turned from me, he would have seen how stressed out the guy looked.

"Agent Tagge, I don't want to be—"

"Lahm," the guy insisted.

He slowly turned from looking at me, finally giving his attention to the other agent. "What the fuck is so crucial that you're interrupting an interrogation?"

"You've got a call from the assistant to the deputy secretary of the DOD holding on line one for you."

It was unexpected, and Efrem took a moment to recover. "I'm sorry."

The agent tipped his head at me. "Apparently we cannot legally hold Mr. Harris."

"Says who?"

"The CIA."

"The CIA has no jurisdiction in the United States."

"No, but apparently he's their guy, and the DOD wants him— and his cohort—out of here right fucking now."

"I—"

"Shit," the agent muttered under his breath as he was shoved sideways as more men in suits and ties filed into the room, finally followed by possibly the prettiest man I'd ever seen in my life, Lee Tae San.

I stood up as Lee swaggered over to the table. There was no other word to describe that walk of his, the kind that ticked you off just seeing it, a strut, imperious, pretentious, smug, all the things that made other men want to take a swing at him. His face didn't help matters, all that perfection, from his delicate bone structure to the knowing grin, to the flawless, poreless skin. When he tossed his head sideways, his thick, glossy black hair moved with him and then settled—like he was animated instead of real—across his forehead.

"Who the hell are you?" Efrem barked.

"Conrad Harris has been released into my custody," Lee informed him, holding out his business card for Efrem to take between two fingers like he was dealing cards at a blackjack table. It was horribly unprofessional, and the smirk was not helping matters. Even the beige suit he was wearing with a white cashmere crew neck sweater underneath was somehow irritating. He looked so much more polished, more pristine, crisper, cleaner than the rest of us.

He was dressed to walk a runway, not spring me from federal custody.

I couldn't help scowling.

"Oh, what now?" he asked, voice swimming in condescension.

I gestured at all of him.

He took hold of the lapels of his suit jacket and checked himself out before lifting his head to scoff at me. "I look great."

I opened my mouth to snap at him, but he tsked to get me to shut up. It was rude and brusque, and I was going to murder him when we got out of the room, but at the moment, I let him hush me as he turned his head to look at Efrem.

My ex was seething as he glared at the just slightly smaller man now regarding him with big innocent eyes. "He's not going anywhere."

"Perhaps you need to talk to the man holding on line one for you," he suggested before glancing around the room. "This is not what I imagined this would look like. How banal."

Efrem growled before charging from the room.

"You," Lee snapped at Tagge, who was still hovering at the door. "Come unlock him before I ruin your career as well."

"Pardon me."

"And that suit is atrocious," Lee said, grimacing like he was in pain. "Really, how bourgeois."

"Jesus," I muttered as Tagge, even dealing with the insults, scrambled to do what Lee ordered, neither his tone or facial expressions giving the man pause.

Ten minutes later, after collecting my things—including Trevan—I was standing outside the building with Lee, him there with his hands shoved down into the pockets of his white wool topcoat, and me, arms crossed, glowering at him.

"Are you mad?" Trevan asked me, shifting from foot to foot, clearly freezing in the frigid March air.

"Yes, I'm mad," I said, gesturing at Lee. "He made that so much more difficult than it needed to be!"

"Are you kidding?" Trevan said, clearly in awe. "He was awesome."

Lee crossed his arms too, rocking back on his heels and waggling his perfectly straight eyebrows at me. "You see? I'm awesome."

I shook my head. "Where's the car?"

As we walked, I realized how old I felt. Not just because sometimes old injuries—far too many to count—ached, especially in the cold, but mainly because with Trevan at twenty-six and Lee at twenty-five, I really *was* positively ancient at forty-five.

Lee had brought a tricked-out Chevy Suburban, and when the three of us got in, the two bodyguards in front were cut off from us by a partition that slid shut.

I stared out the window as I heard Lee and Trevan introducing themselves and talking, Lee telling him how much he was going to love the club scene in Boston.

"So Dari—"

I cleared my throat.

"Conrad," Trevan corrected himself. Lee didn't know the name, and would not, "told you that me and my husband were moving to Boston with him?"

"He did," Lee said quickly, his deep, husky voice a nice counterpoint to Trevan's gruff honeyed tone. Just listening to them chat was like salve on an open wound. "I'm the one who found the building down on Newbury Street that you and your husband will be living out of and that he'll have his shop in."

"Oh, thank you."

I was sure that Lee had noticed the stop and start in conversation—the man missed nothing—but he didn't ask. He probably didn't care enough to inquire. Things that didn't affect him directly were seldom of any interest.

"When I spoke to Landry yesterday, he told me that the space was exquisite."

"You saw him?"

"I did. He can't wait for you to get there."

I turned my chin to look at Trevan.

He was studying Lee. "Did he look all right? He's been there for a week already, and we Facetime every night, but—he normally shows me the street and how the work on the gallery's coming along but not, you know, him."

Lee thought for a moment. "He looks tired, and he must have said your name a hundred times in our ten-minute conversation, but he looked fine to me."

Trevan exhaled deeply. "Okay, good."

"We're going from here to the airport," Lee announced with a grin, turning to me in that way he had that was overly done, like a bobblehead, so I couldn't miss it. "Both of your bags are in the back."

Trevan had said his goodbyes to his mother and sisters the night before, and they promised to visit the following weekend to see his and Landry's new place. It was an hour and twenty or so minute flight between cities, and the airfare was cheap. They would have no trouble staying in touch. And with Trevan gone, out of the picture and out of Detroit, they were no longer on anyone's radar. Not that I'd found the mob to ever be particularly bloodthirsty when it came to revenge on family members. Held for leverage, yes; killed outright, no. And since there was nothing anyone needed from Trevan, his family was off-limits as per the unwritten laws of mob honor. He himself, that was another story, hence my inclusion of him on my master list when I became the vault.

"Hello."

I realized Lee had asked me a question that I'd totally blown off, lost as I was in thought. "What?"

"Are you going to tell me who that man was?"

"What man?"

"The one looking at you like a lover and not as a suspect?"

"Who was this?" Trevan wanted to know.

I groaned and turned back to the window. "Someone I used to know that clearly, I don't anymore."

"Ah, so, what then, if I see him skulking around should I shoot him?" Lee asked.

"You don't shoot anyone anymore," I said snidely, "you have people to do that."

"Don't kid yourself. I still kill lots of people."

That was probably true, but I baited him anyway because I could. "No," I taunted, "you don't want to get dirty."

Something in Korean then that I knew was *not* complimentary, and he shut up.

"Are you not friends?" Trevan asked.

Lee scoffed, I snorted out a laugh, and then we went back to being silent.

CHAPTER FOUR

As SOON as I became the vault, the first thing I did was go to Boston—and from there out to Nahant—to speak with Ceaton Mercer and convince him to become my knight. The second thing on my list was to go to New Orleans, where I knew Lee Tae San was visiting, to deliver the good news to him in person.

He was eating at one of my favorite places, Mr. B's Bistro down on Royal Street, having the barbecue shrimp I loved, when I took a seat across from him.

"This is brave of you," he said cheerfully, always with the smirk, on the whole patronizing me as he let out a long, bored sigh.

I leaned back and grinned. "So guess who just became the vault?"

His eyes, deep chestnut brown framed with long thick lashes, flicked up from his food to my face.

"Care to venture a guess?"

He grunted as he squared his shoulders before putting down his fork and knife. "Why do I care about this?"

"I dunno. Why do you think?"

He laced his fingers together and leaned forward, resting his chin on the bridge he'd made as he stared at me. "It's the perfect job for you, Harris. Sedentary, quiet, anonymous but for a few people… makes perfect sense to me. This way you won't throw out a hip or something running around and jumping off buildings."

He was such an ass.

"You're not as young as you used to be; you should leave the killing to me."

Lee Tae San was, at the moment, without a doubt, the best assassin in the world. Born to middle-class working parents in

Seoul, he looked like the kind of guy who should have been singing K-pop or acting in film or TV, but instead, after graduating from Myongji University at twenty-one, he went into the Army to fulfill his mandatory federal service and found out something interesting about himself. He really enjoyed shooting a gun. After almost two years, he was out and went to work with a friend who was having some trouble with a criminal element. After Lee took care of that trouble, permanently and with prejudice, no one bothered his friend again. The word was out: don't try to blackmail or extort money from anyone Lee knew because, gun or knife, no one wanted to cross him.

Slowly, steadily, Lee built a reputation for being methodical, dangerous, and difficult. If someone who lived at Fort Knox needed killing, Lee was the guy called. He was brilliant and frightening and, between what he looked like and how peacefully and without pain most of his victims were dispatched, he was christened with the name Angel. Not Angel of Death, nothing ominous, simply that, simply Angel.

As he sat across from me, I could certainly vouch for him having the looks of a heavenly creature.

His skin was silky, flawless ivory perfection with warm cream undertones, and his features, while not feminine in the least, were still delicately carved, with a short, straight nose and soft pink lips. What made him different from the other stunningly beautiful Korean men I'd met in my life were his eyebrows. He had the most expressive eyebrows that he used dramatically to show off surprise, irritation, and disapproval. That was the one I got the most. He was forever looking at me as though he'd just bitten into a lemon or was judging me for some stupid thing I'd said or done. It was that part that drove me nuts.

"Can't."

"What?" he asked, having gone back to eating while I was thinking about him.

"You said that I should leave the killing to you, but I can't."

Quick flashing grin. "And why's that?"

"Because you work for me now."

The choke was fast, some coughing before he righted himself. "You need to see a doctor. Your dementia is progressing."

I shook my head. "No, I get to choose my second, as the vault, and I choose you to fly all over the world and collect things for me so I can sit on my ass at home and read."

His eyes narrowed.

"Just think, you go everywhere on me, you get to network, you get to kill people on occasion, and you know secrets that no one else will."

He took a sip of whatever white wine he was drinking with his shrimp. It smelled good, fruity.

"And best of all, I could die, and you'd get to tell everyone. Doesn't that sound great?"

"You dying sounds marvelous, but why in the world would you pick me?"

Because he was smart, instinctive, hyperaware of his surroundings, detail-oriented, could charm the hell out of anyone— given his superlative interpersonal skills with everyone but me— and was both quick to discern the motives of those around him and deadly, making him the perfect combination for the position I needed him in. Ceaton, my knight, was the opposite. He could be engaging if he tried, but mostly he was loyal and protective and laser-focused on my safety, which was why there was no one better for that job.

"Hello," he flared angrily, snapping his fingers in my face. "Wake up, old man."

"I will break your hand if you don't move it."

"Oh, how frightening."

I was having second thoughts. I could just wring his neck right there and find a bishop I didn't want to throttle.

"So?" he demanded before muttering something under his breath in Korean. "Why me?"

"Because no one's ever going to think you're the bishop of the vault, with that pretty face of yours."

The scowl was instant.

"What?"

"Suddenly I have no skills, I'm just pretty?"

"Is that what I said?"

"I—"

"Besides," I said with a shrug. "Your mother thought it was a great idea. She worries, you know, with you killing people and all."

His mouth dropped open.

I had to hand it to him. Most guys would not have had the balls to tell their parents that their only child was a contract killer. But Lee Tae San had told them because he didn't lie to them. Never had, was not about to start now. If he couldn't do something without them knowing, then it wasn't worth doing. It was impressive, and I'd used it to my advantage.

"You talked to my mother?"

I nodded.

"You went to Seoul," he pried, eyes narrowing, and I knew why. He was trying to catch me in a lie. We both knew where his parents were.

"Actually," I said, calling his bluff, knowing he was trying to trick me. "Your folks were vacationing in Rome when I caught up with them."

"I will kill you for this."

I scoffed. "You will not."

His gaze locked on mine.

"I'm saving your life, man."

"And how do you figure that?"

"It's no life for a man who's supposed to get married and have kids someday."

"You—"

"That's what your mother said."

He sat there staring at me.

"Just think about your own private plane. You can have orgies in the sky."

He was not amused.

"You get paid a lot, just think of all the clothes you can buy. Women love a sharp-dressed man."

Still nothing.

"Are you going to eat that?" I asked, reaching for his lunch.

He blocked me but called over the waiter and asked him to bring me the same thing he was having.

"We're eating now?"

"Do I have security clearances?"

"Yes."

"Do I get military-grade tech?"

"Yes."

"May I have a gun made?"

"Yes."

He nodded. "And if you die, am I out?"

"If you want."

He was thinking.

"I could get shot tomorrow and make your whole year," I pointed out.

His face brightened; clearly this was good news.

"So?"

He pushed his wineglass over to me. "Try this Gewürztraminer, it's really good. I like the Trimbach more than others I've had."

He was like an evil imp, and I wasn't buying it. "We're not friends."

"No," he agreed. "But is that what you need?"

It wasn't, no.

"Try the wine."

It was good. I ordered my own glass with my shrimp.

NOW, AS I sat beside him in the back of the Chevy Suburban, I realized that in just a very short time, I'd come to depend upon him as a confidant, a fixer, and most of all, as an ally. He was still scary, but his loyalties were clear. He was, most definitely, my man. Friends we were not, but it was inching decidedly in that direction despite what either of us wanted.

"So?" Lee began, smirking at me. "Am I to shoot that man if I see him again or no?"

"No."

"No?"

"Just—leave it alone."

His gaze was on me, heavy, trying to peek inside. "Why?"

"It's nothing to concern yourself with."

"An agent from Homeland Security took you in, and then the DOD springs you on the word of the CIA, and I show up to collect you, and you think, what, he's just going to drop it?"

It sounded ridiculous when he said it like that.

"Do you need to lie down?"

"No, I don't need to—"

"You *are* old."

I wanted to punch him in his smug little face.

"I mean, what are you now, like fifty?"

"He's not fifty," Trevan said quickly before turning to me. "You aren't, are you?"

I pulled my sunglasses from the breast pocket of my suit jacket and put them on quickly.

"I think my dad had some like that," Lee offered, smiling at me. "Those are Ray Bans right, the Clubmaster? The partial metal rim is really old school."

He was lucky I wasn't strapped.

"I'll be in Boston next week."

I needed him to stop talking. I needed to drop Trevan off with Landry, and I needed to drive out to my new house on Nahant and just have some quiet time to reflect upon seeing Efrem Lahm. I needed to process that whole encounter.

It had gone nothing like I'd thought it would. Never in my wildest dreams had I imagined that Efrem would choose his job over me if actually given the choice.

"Are you listening to me?"

I turned my head to him.

"I was saying that I have to fly to Cairo tonight and then go to Amsterdam on Thursday."

It was only Monday; he was going to have a busy week. I forced a smile. "Well, that will be good. Amsterdam, I mean, you like blondes."

"I do, so the Netherlands is a good place to start."

"Have you been there a lot?" Trevan asked him.

"A few times," Lee answered. "You and Landry should come with me some time."

They started talking then, and I was glad to not be included, old man that I was.

CHAPTER FIVE

I WAS surprised to see Ceaton there to greet me when Trevan and I landed at Logan Airport. His text came through as we were getting off the plane, and as we waited for our luggage, I saw him and Pravi walk toward us.

When I'd first asked Ceaton to be my backup, to lead the team that protected me, I'd thought that I'd only ever see him. I'd thought that the guys who worked for him wouldn't be familiar faces in my life. What I hadn't counted on, though, was how close Ceaton already was with the men he worked with. They were more than coworkers. They were family, and so what had started out so very structured—I had a military background, so that only made sense—deteriorated in a very short time. Normally that would have bothered me. I had a finite number of people in the world who knew me, who I cared about, but lately that number was growing, and I wasn't sure how comfortable I was with that yet.

What I did know was that I liked being met in the baggage claim, and seeing Ceaton soothed me for the simple reason that I considered him a friend. It was a strange feeling.

I returned Ceaton's wave as Trevan slipped from behind me to my side.

"Who are they?"

"The bigger guy is Ceaton," I told him. "You've heard me talk about him before."

"Yeah, but who's the other guy?"

Pravi Radic was the guy prowling beside my number two, moving with a sort of boneless quality that made people watch him walk by. He oozed sex appeal, that raw, dirty kind that said he'd be good in bed. But also, lingering around his eyes, was just enough of a trace of vulnerability to make keeping him a keen, sharp desire. Pravi was a wicked temptation from his deep-set eyes to his full lush lips, and he had a way of grinning that made both women and men ready to drop to their knees. I'd never had that effect on anyone. I'd always been the scariest guy in the room.

"Darius?"

I cleared my throat, realizing that because I'd seen Efrem, I was suddenly thinking about sex. Players like Pravi didn't do it for me, but the fact that I was noticing how well his suit fit was a clear indication I wasn't really seeing him. The itch I had could only be scratched by one man, and seeing him had reminded me of lust and longing.

"Darius?" Trevan asked again.

"Sorry," I huffed. "That's Pravi, he's Ceaton's guy."

"His boyfriend?"

"No, they're friends, and they work together."

"Got it."

"I never see you notice other men."

Trevan gestured at Pravi. "You'd have to be blind not to see him, but you know me, Landry's the only one I give a shit about."

It was so very true. Trevan would take a bullet for his husband at a moment's notice, if needed. I'd never seen two people so in love, though, it was a kind of love I didn't understand. At times, over the years, I had worried about Trevan and had dropped in unannounced to see him. I'd told him that watching him sleep soothed me, that sometimes just breathing the same air did, but that was a lie. I'd been there to check on him, to make sure that Landry's possessiveness had not turned deadly. I made more excuses to come and go, letting Trevan think I myself could hurt him and so was leaving instead of turning my homicidal urges on him. It was crap. I had no impulse control issues; I was a contract killer, for the love of God, and really, if he'd thought about it logically, he would have known all of that was an excuse to come and go without having my motives questioned. I'd told him he was special, and that was true, but not for any other reason than he was my friend.

I watched Landry sometimes when I knew he wasn't looking, and I'd watch him stare at Trevan. It wasn't hungry or predatory, it wasn't fanatical or scary. He looked at Trevan with absolute focus as though he were the only thing in the world. It wasn't that Landry didn't love Trevan—he did, completely, with his whole heart, with everything in him—but there was that little bit extra I didn't like and was the reason that still, I checked on Trevan.

He said that sometimes one thought got stuck in Landry's mind, and no matter what he did, he couldn't stop the fixation, couldn't pull himself loose until something, or someone, jostled him. Trevan was very good at picking him up, dusting him off, and putting him back on track. There was patience in him, even with how young he was, that I had never possessed. Being the best man at their wedding a year ago had felt a bit hypocritical because, while I knew Trevan loved Landry and Landry loved Trevan, I still felt a twinge of concern as the marriage had been a source of contention for more than a year. Trevan worried that his life was so uncertain, it was unfair to ask to bind Landry to him. Landry, in his regular style, gave Trevan an ultimatum.

I was there, at their apartment, dropping Trevan off after work when we both noticed the open window leading out to the fire escape. Leaning out, I saw Landry, beautiful blond-maned Landry with his wild dark blue eyes, sitting on the edge of the roof of the building next door. And it wasn't so much where he was sitting, but how. He was perched there; legs draped over the side, like he could scoot forward and plummet to his death. I was going to yell when my phone rang.

I put it on speaker and answered roughly, my voice stumbling on the words. "Hey Lan, what are you doing?"

"Is Trevan there?"

"Of course I am," Trevan answered softly.

"Are you home yet?"

"Yeah."

"Can you see me?"

"Yes."

"Trevan," he said, sounding like he was drugged.

"Hey baby," he soothed, always when he spoke to Landry, the love and tenderness right there on the tip of his tongue.

"You're being so selfish," he explained, staring at Trevan across the chasm separating them. "I want to get married, you want to get married, but you're worried that maybe you're going to die and leave me all alone."

"I am worried about that," Trevan agreed.

"You need to stop already," he informed him, "because you know that if anything ever happened to you, I'd be right behind you."

Trevan swallowed hard. "But I'd want you to live, baby."

"Oh no, no, no, no," Landry sighed. "There's no me without you. Not ever. So you have to stop concerning yourself with that, all right?"

"Okay," Trevan allowed.

"The only reason for not wanting to marry me would be that you just don't want to because you don't love me," he said wearily, and even from the distance I could see that he'd been crying.

"That's bullshit, and you know it," Trevan insisted, climbing out the window and onto the fire escape, leaning over, the railing pressing into his abdomen as he spread his arms. "Now get the fuck down and come over here before I slip and fall," he yelled over at Landry.

From looking like he was halfway dead, as though a stiff wind could blow him off the ledge, I watched Landry scramble back and down onto the roof, shrieking at the top of his lungs for Trevan to be careful.

"It's rusty!" he yelled, and I could hear him bumping down stairs because the phone call was still live. "Trevan, ohmygod!"

Always, always, Trevan knew what to do where Landry was concerned. I could not have done it, wrapped my life around someone that delicate, that unhinged, his grasp on reality at times so tenuous that it was breakable by a glance.

The call went dead, and Trevan rose, turned, and leaned back against the railing, the weight of his carved muscular frame causing the dated metal to groan.

Landry came in fast, hurling open the front door, tossing his phone on the couch as he ran by and charged over to Trevan, leaping at the last minute without thinking that his added weight might break the railing and send them both to their deaths with the sudden jolt.

Trevan, though, always thinking, had levered off the rail at the last moment and caught Landry as he flung himself into his arms. They stood there together, Trevan holding him as Landry coiled around him tight.

"Don't do that again," Trevan warned.

His face buried against Trevan's shoulder, Landry only nodded.

"We'll get married on Friday, all right? We'll go get rings tonight."

Landry lifted his face, streaked with tears, and Trevan leaned in and kissed him. I started for the door then.

"You have to stand up and be my best man on Friday, okay?" Trevan called out.

I nearly tripped because, Jesus, this kid and his surprises. "You sure you want me?" I asked, not turning around as I neared the doorway.

"I want you," Trevan assured me.

"Me too," Landry added before I heard only the sound of kissing behind me.

I closed the door on my way out, making sure it was locked.

"Maybe you and Pravi, huh?"

I jolted out of my memories back to the present. Turning, I regarded Trevan. "What?"

"What?" he asked me.

"What are you talking about?"

He leaned closer. "I know you're gay, you told me."

"Oh, for fuck's sake," I groaned, not even going to try to explain to him that Pravi was straight and that even if he wasn't, I was not interested beyond looking. Sadly, my body didn't go where my heart didn't lead, so one-night stands or short-term anything were not for me. The whole international playboy thing other murder-for-hire guys I knew had going on—Lee, for example—had never been me. I hadn't slept my way across Europe or anywhere else. Before Efrem Lahm, a handful of guys, nothing serious, nothing lasting, and after him, no one. It was just how I was made. I was not about to get on board with having one-night stands now.

"I think you need to start dating."

I *needed* to rest, take a real vacation, get away from everyone and everything. I couldn't remember ever doing nothing in my entire adult life.

"Boss," Ceaton said as he stepped in front of me.

I sighed, then groaned without meaning to.

"What's the matter?" Ceaton asked quickly.

"Nothing, sorry."

"Who's this?" Pravi asked, glancing at Trevan.

"He's the one I told you about," I informed them. "I sent you to find a place for his Cuban restaurant, and you found one over in Faneuil Hall."

"It's in a hall?" Trevan chimed in.

"No, it's actually Faneuil Hall Marketplace, but no one says marketplace here," I explained.

"I get it," Trevan said with a smile. "So, you guys know the area, I don't. Is that a good place for a restaurant?"

"It is," Pravi assured him. "It's near the Garden for basketball and hockey, and also close to the waterfront."

"So, good, then?"

Ceaton nodded. "Very good, and you'll only be like twenty minutes, give or take, from your home down on Newbury, which I understand is important as well."

"Yeah," Trevan sighed.

"So you want to see it?" Ceaton asked.

He glanced at me. "I do, but I need to go check on Landry first."

"Of course," I agreed, turning to Ceaton. "Could you take Trevan home and then take him and his husband over to see the space for the restaurant?"

"I can have Luka and Marko take them. Pravi and I are here to take you home."

I shook my head. "I parked a car here. You guys go do that, I'm good."

Ceaton scowled at me.

"It's fine."

"May I speak to you a moment?"

I didn't realize how really dead tired I was until I followed him a few feet away. "You're being ridiculous," I chided Ceaton.

He rounded on me. "I thought you said that Trevan's old boss was gunning for you."

"There's always someone looking to put holes in me," I explained. "You know this."

"Yeah, but this guy Fanton sounds particularly pissed off."

"He's madder at Trevan, but I'm not worried about that."

"Why?"

"Trevan's on my list with the vault."

"Oh," he said, nodding.

"And so are you by the way."

His head snapped up. "What?" he asked, breathless.

"Oh, I surprised you," I said, grinning at him. "I didn't think I could."

"How did—you just put me on your list without knowing if I'd say yes or no to you?"

"Yes."

"Why?"

"Because even if you said no, it was still the right thing to do, to protect you long-term, and save you from Grigor in the short."

He cleared his throat. "Thank you."

"You're very welcome," I assured him. "Hey, how did you get here so fast?"

"I left Detroit when I saw you and Trevan get picked up by whoever that was."

"Homeland."

"For what?"

"They weren't sure who Trevan was moving guns for, if he had ties to terrorists."

"But Trevan doesn't move guns."

"That's what I said."

Ceaton grunted.

"So you left as soon as you saw us get picked up? Why?"

"I got a call from Lee and he said they were legit law enforcement, so that took me out of the equation and put him in play."

I nodded. "Yes, it did."

"I figured you'd want me back here keeping things secure."

"Yes, smart. Thank you."

"You do realize that I'd never have left you if I thought you were in any—"

"I know."

We stood there, staring at each other for several heartbeats.

"So," I sighed, "did you take care of that issue for me?"

"Modella?" Ceaton asked, squinting.

I nodded.

"I dealt with him the day you mentioned your concern."

"And?"

"And you don't need to know where all the bodies are buried."

He was right, I didn't. "Thank you," I said as my phone buzzed. "He hurt a friend, as I told you. It took me longer than I thought it would to find him."

"Who's calling you?" he asked, not interested in the least in talking about Esau Modella, the man who had nearly killed my friend Duncan a few years back.

I checked the display. "Oh, it's Daoud. I told him I'd be here later today. He probably wants to see me." I said, texting back my reply and waiting a moment before I got his in return.

"I'll go with you. Pravi can take care of Trevan and Landry himself."

I shook my head, answering again, arranging a time and place to meet my old colleague. "I'll be fine. Please, take care of them. They need to know they have a network here."

Ceaton shot me a pained look.

"I promise you, Trevan will be an asset. He's always been one to me."

"And his boyfriend?"

"Husband," I corrected.

"Husband," he parroted.

What to say about Landry. "As long as Trevan's good, he's good," I said.

He looked wary, unsure.

"When you meet him, you'll get it."

He was still eyeing me.

"I'm going home," I told him.

He opened his mouth to argue.

"Take care of Trevan and Landry. Call me tomorrow."

I could tell he wanted to argue, but I was done, too tired to even debate with him. I just wanted to sit and not think at all.

FORTY MINUTES later—the traffic was murder—I was on Nahant, on my way home when I stopped close to Tudor Wharf because I recognized my neighbor Sousanna Bath leaning on the railing, eyes closed, head raised, like she was taking a deep breath of the salty air. The fact that she lived next to me on Ocean Street and was not anywhere near there was not what concerned me. It was her outfit. She was wearing flannel pajamas under a long down-filled parka with a really ugly hat, the kind with the earflaps, wedge snow boots, and she was smoking a cigarette. All this in the middle of the day alone made it impossible for me to drive by. I was in my Lexus GX 460, which I'd left at the airport, wanting to drive home in my own SUV instead of taking a cab or having someone ferry me out here. Pulling up beside her, I turned on the hazards, left the motor running, got out, and moved to her side.

"Sous," I greeted her.

She sighed deeply before turning her head to blow smoke away from me and then smiling wide when she was back to looking at me. "Darius, good to see you."

It was still strange to hear that name from anyone other than Efrem, but I'd told first Ceaton, as well as his boyfriend, Brinley Todd, and Ceaton's guys, then my neighbor. I hadn't told Lee. He was still using Conrad, which I actually preferred with him. It sort of mirrored our relationship, still a bit prickly and mostly professional.

I cleared my throat. "You need a ride home?"

"Yes, that would be really nice. I just have to watch for a few more minutes."

"What?"

She tipped her head, and I glanced out to see a sailboat engulfed in flames.

"Holy crap."

She scoffed.

Eyes back on her. "Sweetheart, is that your boat?"

"It's Dean's boat."

I looked back. "Can I ask why we're watching Dean's boat burn in the harbor?"

"Can you see the piano from here?"

"No, I… no."

She passed me a pair of opera glasses from her pocket.

Once I could see the boat up close, I spotted the living room table I'd taken note of the last time I was in her house, along with the aforementioned grand piano, a lot of suits, some golf clubs, and a portrait of her and her hubby taken by a celebrity photographer years before after they won it at an auction benefiting a children's hospital.

"I liked that table," I commented.

"I liked it, too, but that was before I came home from taking the dogs to the vet and found him fucking my friend Heather on top of it."

"Oh shit."

"Well said," she sighed. "Can you see the metal box?"

"Yeah, what is—oh no." I groaned loudly. "You did not."

"Oh, I did too." She cackled.

I had to smile; it was just too good. "You had the car compacted first?"

She sighed happily.

Her husband, Dean Bath, had shown me the Mercedes-Benz SLR McLaren Roadster 722 S just once. I didn't get to ride in it; I only got to look at it. That was all right. I liked cars, especially fast ones, but I didn't collect them. I didn't idolize them like he did. It had been nice of him to take the time to show me at all; otherwise, I wouldn't have known what I was looking at just from seeing a piece of the fender.

"Holy shit, Sous, he's going to murder you."

"Hah!" She cackled again. "He can try."

I lowered the glasses. "At least now you can do the remodeling in the house you wanted to do without any interference."

"Oh, you're right," she agreed. "Another bonus I hadn't considered. Thank you."

"Not that I don't appreciate the level of retribution that went into this, but won't you get in trouble?"

"Already did," she said, pulling a neatly folded in half white 4x6 piece of paper from her pocket. Once I opened it, I saw that I was looking at a town-issued ticket, not a state one, a Uniform Citation that listed the maritime law for littering and the town laws for open fires. The fine amount was a hundred and fifty dollars and was written out by the harbormaster.

I looked up at her. "That's it?"

"Bill had to do something, even if we are friends, so yes, that's it."

"Did he just notice the fire?"

"No, I called him, and the Coast Guard, to let them know what was going on. Didn't want anyone diverted from something important."

"No, of course not, very thoughtful of you."

She grunted.

"And what happens when it's all burned up?"

"I already made arrangements with a lobsterman to tow it in." She sighed, and then her face lit up. "I didn't want to just leave the carcass out there. I don't want any kids to get the bright idea to go mess around with it."

"Makes sense."

"You're never going to guess what I used for accelerant."

"You didn't just use gasoline?"

"No, that would have been bad for the fish. So would kerosene, so I used all that gin we had left over from the New Year's Eve party."

"That was a lot of gin, and it was in those gallon jugs."

"And you said I'd never have a use for it."

"Well, you showed me."

"Yes, see, even distraught, I'm a friend to the environment."

"Very thoughtful of you," I confirmed as I passed the ticket back, and she gently refolded it and put it in her pocket. "From how careful you're being, I'm thinking you have plans for that."

"Indeed I do," she said cheerfully. "I'm going to frame it and hang it over the toilet in the master bathroom."

I nodded. "Okay. Remind me never to piss you off."

Shifting her weight, she leaned against me. "No, I already know you're not the kind to cheat or break hearts. You're a good man, Darius Hawthorne."

She didn't know anything about me at all, but the words were kind. "Where is ole Dean?"

"In the Bahamas on a business trip."

"He didn't see you? He doesn't know you know?"

"Nope," she assured me, dropping the cigarette and grinding it under her boot before bending to pick it back up. The woman was not a litterbug. Burn all or most of her husband's belongings on his prized sailboat—yes. Leave a cigarette butt on the side of the road—no.

"How does he not know?"

"I came in through the backyard because I left the dogs out there—they always have to go after the vet—and there he was, and there she was, and you know, I always have my phone."

I turned to her. "Did you take video?"

Quick nod.

"What did you—are you—planning to do with it?"

"I met with his partner, Heather's husband, this morning and we commiserated over breakfast, and then we both went home."

I nodded. "Was he sad? Did he cry?"

"No. He did call his lawyer, though. Apparently they had a fidelity clause in their prenup."

"So he's off the hook."

She grunted.

I faced her. "May I drive you home now before you freeze to death?"

"Darling, I don't think I could freeze on Everest in this coat."

"So is that a no on letting me drive you?"

"No, but could we get coffee on the way?"

"Yes, dear."

I got a tender smile in response.

"Did you by any chance meet Heather's husband in this outfit?"

A big impish grin accompanied much nodding.

"What was he wearing?"

"About the same, except, you know, wool cashmere blend overcoat."

"Okay."

I put her in my SUV.

"Oh, I like this," she said, leaning back, getting comfortable. "It was cold outside."

"I thought you said—"

"On my face," she clarified

It was. March in Nahant was still arctic, and she'd been outside for God knew how long.

"You realize they'll be talking about this for years down at the Dunkin' Donuts." She cackled. "Going to be fabulous."

I had liked her the moment I met her, shoveling her driveway after I moved in. She had pointed out another new neighbor on the other side of me.

"Where are you from?" she had asked as I shoveled my own drive, both of us in parkas and boots, gloves, scarves, and wool beanies.

"Detroit," I answered as I moved to shake her hand.

She giggled and asked if I wanted to bet her how long the guy from Jacksonville was going to last in his jeans, sweater, sneakers, and leather jacket. His gloves looked like the kind my mother used to garden, not at all made for warmth.

"That's mean," I said, even as I took that action.

I won hot chocolate at her house when Florida ran inside before he turned into a Popsicle. The two of us helped dig out his Mini Cooper afterward. I explained the benefits of an SUV all-wheel drive and Sousanna explained where the North Face store was downtown. The man at least needed a decent jacket.

We rolled through Dunkin' Donuts, got large coffees, and were home in time for her to meet the locksmith. I waved before I hit the alarm code on my front door and had my hand on the knob when a car pulled into my driveway. I was surprised when Rahm Daoud got out of the oddly colored Ferrari Enzo.

"What the hell is that color?"

He turned and looked at the car he'd just gotten out of before giving me back his attention. "Pearl."

"It's not good," I assured him.

He squinted and tipped his head back and forth like, maybe.

"Are you coming in?"

I didn't have to ask him twice.

CHAPTER SIX

"YOU KNOW," Daoud began once he was sitting at my kitchen table with a cup of Earl Grey tea with milk and honey in his hand, "becoming the vault doesn't suddenly replace God knows how many years of murder-for-hire. You're still you."

"Meaning what?" I asked, yawning as we sat in the kitchen nook off the cavernous kitchen that was better suited to a caterer than me. It was way more than I needed. The double ovens and Gaggenau and Thermador appliances, the skylights, the way the open floor plan flowed from one room to the next—it was stunning. I needed about eight more people living with me in the Tudor-style mansion, though. It was much too big. Though, this way, heaven forbid, if I was ever attacked, I had room to maneuver.

"You're not some paragon of virtue," Daoud pointed out, sipping his tea, squinting at the space around him.

"I never said I was sin-free."

He eyed me. "Just because you're the vault doesn't make you good or any more likely not to go to hell."

"We're carpooling, I'm aware."

He took another sip. "I hate Boston," he informed me.

"Yes, I know, you said that the last time you were here," I reminded him.

"Did I?"

I grunted.

"This house is ridiculous," he said, offhand.

"Says the man who owns a villa on Lake Como," I shot back.

He grunted because, really, there was no comeback to that.

As he stared out at the bay—the view was outstanding—I studied the deep obsidian eyes accentuated by long glossy lashes beneath thick coal brows and thought, as I always did, how striking he was. His gaze, combined with the warm tan skin and jet-black hair, made it difficult for him to go unnoticed, which in our business was problematic. I blended in far easier than he did, and no one had ever told me that being a black man in what, at least in Hollywood, was thought of as exclusively a white man's game, would have seemed problematic. The truth was I'd never been looked at twice whether in Rome or Madrid, Berlin or Paris. Even at six four, built more like a quarterback than a lineman, as Trevan had told me, I went unnoticed in most arenas. I did not stand out. No one had ever told me I didn't *belong* some place, and when people did take a second look at me, it was the bespoke suits, designer shoes, or the Cartier watch that they saw. I came and went more under the radar than most people I knew.

"Where is your head?" he asked, returning his onyx gaze to me.

"I was just thinking how much easier James Bond would blend in if he were black."

He nodded. "It's true. The world is a multicultural place wherever you look."

"Unless you're killing people in rural Kentucky or something," I said snidely, arching an eyebrow to bait him.

"Do shut up."

"How many deputies did that sheriff have again?"

"I can't seem to recall."

I scoffed. "Sometimes if a contract seems odd, you ask a friend to help you out."

He didn't reply, and I went back to admiring the fine aquiline nose and his square jawline that only comic book characters had.

His low chuckle was a surprise.

"What?"

"I see you looking at me like you do."

It was not a secret that I found him alluring, but I had my ridiculous heart to consider, where the fucking had to equal loving. And really, any way you sliced it, sleeping with a man who could kill me was far too deadly a proposition.

"It happens," I granted.

"You're not exactly plain yourself."

I made a sound that was somewhere between a grunt and sigh.

"I've never met anyone with chartreuse-colored eyes in my life. I thought they were odd contacts you wore when I first met you."

"I wear brown ones; you've seen me with them in."

"I have, yes, and while your point is well made that in our melting pot of a world, you fit in even better than Bond, you really are far too handsome a man to be a secret agent. If you really think about it, they should be utterly plain and forgettable. Whyever would any agency want strikingly gorgeous agents that everyone notices? That's the height of stupidity."

I smiled. "Did you actually just come here to stroke my ego?"

"No," he sighed, slouching in the comfortable wide-backed chair. They were nice, I knew; I'd picked them so I could sit in them for long periods of time. I planned to have a great many chats in my kitchen. "I wanted to tell you that, that guy Eastman upped the cost of the contract out on you."

I nodded. "I figured."

"But more importantly, may I ask a question?"

I was expecting it. "Go ahead."

He leaned close, arms crossed on the table. "Why you?"

"Why not me?" I asked coolly.

"Oh, come on, Con."

Of the contract killers I knew, only he used the shortened version of that name, and somehow, the informality struck me as almost friendly.

I shrugged.

"You won't answer?"

"Do I have to?"

"It's a staggering undertaking, and you're so glib?"

"I'm qualified, am I not?"

"Yes, but the same could be said for many others, for me."

"True."

"Then?"

"Perhaps I'm more connected than you know."

His eyes narrowed as he studied me. "I know everything there is to know about you."

Doubtful.

"Why do you think they chose you? Why were you picked above everyone else to be the vault?"

"Your guess is as good as mine."

"No, really, tell me."

Sitting there across from a man who'd tried to kill me on a number of occasions before we'd come to an understanding, I wasn't sure what to say.

"Well?"

"I was chosen because I'm prettier than you."

His eyes widened almost comically. "That's madness!"

I laughed at him, at how irate he looked.

"So the contract that's out on me, you're not taking the job?" I teased, leaning forward on the table.

His scowl was dark.

"I figured, but I had to ask." I shrugged. "I mean, how smart would it be to come here and then just pull your gun and shoot me."

"As though you would allow that to happen," he said, chuckling.

There was that.

"Is that new guy I met last time around here somewhere?"

"His name's Mercer."

"Yes, Mercer. Not pretty, lots of muscles, not much else."

"You'd be surprised," I said, defending the man I'd hired to watch my back. I was already becoming friends with him. If the men who trained me could see this new softer side of me, they would have gagged. A contract killer with friends was counterintuitive, though truly, that wasn't me anymore.

"He's not nearly as smooth as you, my friend," Daoud said, reminding me that we were having a conversation.

"Not many men are," I replied, my tone silvery, dipped in honey.

His lips parted, and I heard a small puff of air escape.

"And no, I don't need watching in my new home."

"Meaning that you're not afraid of me?"

"If I was, I would have never told you where I lived in the first place."

"Really?"

I crossed my arms. "Are we not friends?"

"Are we?"

"We are."

"When did that happen?"

"I think a long time ago, back when I needed that gun planted in that rental car in Vegas a few years ago."

It took him a second. "Are you kidding? That was nothing."

"You were the only one close enough to help me, and I needed a piece. It was a big thing, make no mistake."

He leveled a stare at me. "So, now that you're the vault, what name are you going by?"

"Harris."

"That makes sense; it's what you used to build your dangerous reputation, might as well trade on it."

"That was my thought, but alone, with friends, I'm using my real name, Darius Hawthorne."

"Really?"

"Yes. It's time to make a change and put my faith in people. I've been so suspicious for so long and of course," I said, thinking of Efrem and how disappointed I was, "mostly for good reason. But it's time to trust those who have proven themselves over and over again."

His eyes didn't leave me.

"So if you would be so kind as to call me by the name my mother christened me with, I would be grateful."

"I would be honored," he said hoarsely.

I dipped my head.

"And you, please, use Rahm, not my last name."

"Agreed."

We were quiet for long minutes, both of us letting the gravity of the situation sink in. We weren't going to be icy to each other anymore. No more civility, only something real and important and final.

"You know, if you're dead," he began after taking another sip of his tea. "Then they can take out—what's his name?"

"Trevan."

"Yes, well, if you're dead, then Trevan and his partner and the rest of his family are all on the chopping block."

"Not his family, right? That's not the way the mob generally does things."

"Well, certainly that husband of his. The spouse always goes, too, just not the kids."

I grunted.

"You're not concerned?"

"No."

"And why not?"

"Well, Mercer, as you said," I reminded him. "Plus, I moved them here with me."

"Who?"

"Trevan and his husband."

"Here?"

"Not here, here," I said irritably. "Here to Boston."

"No kidding."

I threw up my hands.

"You know I think it's actually smart, you taking on being the vault, because you're getting damn sentimental."

"I am not!"

He shot me a look that said otherwise.

"I'm practical. You know that."

"Normally."

"Let it go," I warned.

He scoffed. "So, who did Fortney?"

I met his dark gaze. "Mercer."

"That was messy."

"As was the point."

He nodded.

Again we sat in a contented silence, the type you have with those who might not be your closest friends but who respect the hell out of you.

"I called Isaak," he said suddenly like the thought had just hit him.

"To see if he was going to take the contract on me?"

"Yes. He would be the only other person they could ask besides Lee."

"Lee works for me now."

"Really?"

I nodded. "The vault has two specific positions. Mercer has one, him the other."

He smiled. "I'm guessing these are not voluntary."

"Mercer's is, not Lee's."

"That was kind of you not to think of me, thank you."

"You're too entrenched with the Mossad, and I know that's your passion. I'd never ask you to give that up."

His eyes warmed, and I saw it, the shift in him from predator to confidant.

"Lee could be moved on the chessboard."

"Plus he's young and pretty and likes to be seen."

"He does."

"How's the pay?"

"Not what he was getting, but his work was sporadic, so I suspect it will even out, be more in the long run."

"And the perks?"

"He has his own team, and, oh, a plane."

"A plane is good."

I grinned. "You said you called Isaak?"

"I did."

"How? Did you hold a séance or something?"

"What are you talking about?"

"I thought Isaak was dead."

His eyebrows shot up. "Why would you think that?"

"I heard the Russian was dead."

"No, no, no, you always got that fucked up. Isaak isn't the Russian, Evgeni was."

I squinted at him. "Are you sure?"

He rolled his eyes at me.

"So wait, then *Evgeni* is actually dead?"

"Yes. It was that job in Florence."

"Oh, so that's how that went down."

He nodded. "I crossed paths with Isaak in Berlin about a month ago, and I got the whole story from him."

I was surprised. "He talked to you?"

Quick shrug. "He did. He's back to verbal communication again."

I had to think. "He took that vow of silence, what—two years ago?"

Nod.

"That whole thing was weird," I mused.

His scoff made me smile. "At least you didn't have to work with him. We went after that cartel head in Nuevo Leon, and the whole time we're there, not one word."

Imagining it, Isaak all serious, Rahm just wanting some kind of diversion, was hysterical. Stuck together like rats in a cage. "I couldn't use my satellite phone. I was so bored. All I did was smoke pot and eat. And it was the worst kind of weed there, all of the munchies, none of the buzz."

I couldn't stifle my chuckle.

"Anyway, I didn't get ahold of Isaak, so I'll try again."

"Thank you," I sighed.

"You sound sad all of a sudden."

"It's just," I began solemnly, thinking of the man I'd never see again. "I'll miss Zhenya," I murmured, using the familiar form of Evgeni's name. We had been friends of a sort. There had been a mutual regard there, without question.

"Me too," Rahm whispered, leaning back, lifting his cup to mine.

I touched my mug to his, and we drank a silent toast to our friend who had probably been left for dead wherever he fell. Such was the life of a contract killer; there was no one waiting at home to grieve you.

"So," he husked. "I'll talk to Isaak."

"And tell me what he says. I need to know either way if he's coming for me."

He scoffed. "Come on, you know he won't. Imagine what the price would have to be to make him take the job."

"Maybe he's mad at me for something."

"He's not that way, and you know it."

I did, actually.

"Are you on speaking terms with Mancuso?" Rahm asked.

"Oh, don't worry about that, Chris would never take a contract on—"

"No, not that, something else."

"So what's your question?"

"You're friendly with him, right?"

"I am, yes," I replied, not having to give it much thought. I'd known Christopher Mancuso a very long time, longer than I'd known Dante Cerreto, as he and I had been in the same Ranger unit together. "Why, you're not?"

He winced. "We had a misunderstanding over a contract in Mexico City, and now he's all pissy."

"A K&R, or something else?"

"You know me, the last time I fucked around with a K&R situation was the one you and I were on when we pulled that kid out of Afghanistan two years ago."

"Then what was it?"

"It was a thing, a tiny thing."

I squinted at him. "Yes, but everyone knows Mancuso does all the cartel work in the southwest and Mexico. He has since his days with the company. Why would you step in that?"

He winced again.

"What the hell did you do?"

"Why do you just assume it was my fault?" His voice climbed several octaves at once, and I was immediately suspicious.

I glared at him. "Why would you ever get between Chris Mancuso and the cartel?"

"I was right there. I figured it would be quick and easy."

"But? I hear a but."

"He got seriously pissed that I took a contract there and apparently still is."

I scoffed.

"Fuck you, Darius," he said, trying out the new name. "He's taking it so personally, and I have to be in Barcelona next week—"

"Which is where he lives."

"Which is where he lives, yes," he repeated irritably, "and I don't feel like getting my head blown off just walking around because he's still mad."

"So you want me to call him."

"If you would."

"Why are you going to Barcelona?"

"There's a contract out on a billionaire who lives there and I picked it up."

"Who you hope is not one of his friends."

He groaned. "You see? Things like that never crossed my mind before."

"Do you attribute that to age?"

"I attribute that to my colleagues getting very possessive about certain parts of the world."

"Colleagues is a gentle euphemism for people who will kill you."

He grunted.

"But you're talking about Mancuso in Latin America and Mexico and, oddly, Canada."

"Yes."

"And me when I was here and in the Russian Federation."

"What do you mean, when you were here—you're still here."

"Yes, but I'm not going to take contracts anymore. I'm retired. Have been for the past six months."

His brows furrowed.

"You have a question?"

"Yes. Why Russia? Why doesn't Isaak work there, or why did Evgeni exclusively work Eastern Europe and Africa?"

I shrugged. "I think it's wherever you were put by your military originally."

He didn't look convinced.

"You just think I shouldn't be able to get in and out of Russia and Isaak in and out of Haiti and Nigeria."

"Perhaps."

"Because I'm black and he's white, we should be what, reversed?"

"Or maybe since he's Russian, he should, in fact, operate in Russia," he snapped. "It's not a 'color of your skin' thing, it's a 'he was born there and is fluent' thing."

"Again, I think it's the people you get used to seeing and the ones who get used to talking to you."

"I guess so," he agreed, though I didn't delude myself into thinking that I'd convinced him of anything.

"Anyway, I'll talk to Mancuso; make sure he and the billionaire aren't best friends."

"Thank you."

"You don't want to see him, right?"

"No. I just want him to ignore me."

"I'm sure he'll be fine with that."

"Just let me know."

"Before you go?"

"Always such a wiseass," he muttered under his breath. "Do you have anything harder than tea?"

"Yeah, but I don't have any food," I apprised him, sitting up after finding myself sinking into the chair. "You want to go get something to eat?"

He appeared bemused.

"What?"

"You really are going soft. I love the fact that we're eating together all of a sudden."

"Just—don't make a big deal."

"Why not? It's a very friendly thing to do."

It was. "You want Italian? There's a little mom-and-pop Italian place in Swampscott that's amazing, called The Antique Table. You'd like it."

"Whatever you want, I'm game."

Always, even when I'd been contemplating his death, he was still good company. Now that I could let my guard down, putting him in my car was really nice. I could see us making it a habit to see each other and break bread. I had so few friends—a handful, no more—it was terrifying to be adding to the number. Every single time I added a new person, it was like stepping farther out onto a ledge. I used to have a handful of people I could count on. The fact I was now well over double digits in a little over six months was new and dangerous territory.

I let Rahm drive and called Mancuso from the car using the Bluetooth so he could hear.

"Buona Notte Industries," Christopher Mancuso answered on the second ring.

"Chris," I said softly.

"Hold on," he said quickly, hitting a scrambler, I was sure. He always had the best tech. The one I used I'd gotten from him last year. "G'head."

"Hello to you too," I said sarcastically.

"Harris?"

He was being an ass, putting on like he had no idea it was me, when we'd worked together as contractors for years and before that, side by side in the same unit. "If this is how you want this to go, I can—"

"No, shit, sorry," he said with a cough. "I'm in work mode. I'm up to my ears in shit since your buddy Daoud fucked around in my sandbox a few months back."

I panned to Rahm.

"I told you he was mad," he whispered.

"What happened?" I asked innocently.

"He fucked my mark's wife, then when the guy comes up the stairs, he shot him in the head. It was a mess."

I punched Rahm in the bicep.

"Owwww," he whined under his breath.

"What was the fallout?" I asked him, shaking my head at Daoud.

"Well, the police there, we have an understanding, right? I pay them off to look the other way, and as long as it stays neat and tidy and nothing hits the news…we're good."

"But?"

"But this time there was all kinds of news and all kinds of noise and there was DNA *in* the mark's wife as well as all over the bed and—"

"Yes, but none of us have any kind of—"

"Fingerprints and—"

"Again, none us have any identifiable—"

"That's not the point, is it?"

It wasn't, no.

"There are ways that business is transacted, and because he was where he shouldn't have been, now I'm having to mop up bullshit to show that I'm still loyal and that my territory is, in fact, my territory."

"So you had ronin in your territory thinking they could just take contracts?"

"Yeah," he said snidely, "and killing them all has been a pain in the ass."

"They must have thought," I said, staring at Rahm, "that if you were so weak that you let Daoud in then… they could just start back up too."

"Exactly. You don't see me fucking around in his backyard."

"No."

"You don't see me taking contracts in Israel or wherever the hell else he is," Mancuso growled.

"Right."

"Because even though I fuckin' hate him, I respect him, yeah?"

I smacked Rahm on the same arm where I'd punched him.

"I will shoot you," he whispered harshly, reaching for the mirror polish Hard Chrome Kimber 1911 in his shoulder holster that he'd been carrying lately. We used to carry the same gun, but he liked shiny things. I ignored him.

"This is the second time he's done this to me."

"Oh?" I asked Mancuso.

"There was that thing with the Nava Cartel that he fucked around with a few years ago. I could have figured things out between Olivera and Cardoso, but Daoud got in the middle of that one too, and now—he shows up anywhere near my shit again, Harris, and he's a fuckin' dead man. Let him know."

That was clear. "Absolutely."

He huffed out a breath. "Okay, so, you call for anything specific or just to shoot the shit?"

"I have a contract out on me," I said because, while it was true, I knew better.

"You know better'n that," he groused. "You and me are good. Always good."

Funny to hear him use the same words I'd thought seconds earlier. "I figured," I said, exhaling. "Also, I heard there's a contract out on some billionaire in Barcelona. Do you know him?"

"I have a friend in Valencia, not Barcelona, so if I see Isaak on the street before or after, I won't mess with him."

"I didn't think you would," I said, shaking my head at Rahm, who threw up his hands, releasing the wheel for a moment as he did it. The message was clear: Isaak was good to come and go in Mancuso's neck of the woods. Rahm, he'd shoot on sight.

"Hey, is Evgeni really dead?"

"Unfortunately, yes."

"Shit, well. It happens. We'll have to drink to him next time I see you."

I cleared my throat. "Really quick, I have something funny to tell you."

After I was done telling him about the vault and what I wanted to be called, he laughed at me, but it was the nice kind, the warm kind.

"All right, Darius it is."

"Good."

"If you see Daoud, tell him if I see him before he sees me—he's fuckin' dead."

"I would prefer you both to coexist on your opposite ends of the planet."

He grunted.

"I'll keep him out of Spain."

"That would be best."

Once I hung up, I hit Rahm *again*.

"Seriously, vault or no vault, I will shoot you in the head."

"Holy fuckup, Batman," I said seriously, flicking him in the side of the head. He reached for his gun and I swatted him again. "You're really lucky he hasn't shot you."

"Yes, I know, I just—I don't think sometimes."

"I might have made a mistake bringing Lee in instead of you. He actually doesn't need the structure—you do."

"Oh, fuck you."

I slapped his face gently as he parked the car. "Try not to die."

As I got out of the car, he yelled. Not many people got away with hitting Rahm Daoud.

Inside, after we played a lightning-fast round of rock-paper-scissors to see who got to sit facing the door, I was rewarded for the win with hearing some of my favorite stories of his. Of course, this time, when he told the one about him and a deputy US marshal trying to kill each other in a bathroom in an airport in Tennessee, I asked to hear why he thought ever talking to Lior Cardoso in the first place was a good idea. It was good to have teachable moments.

CHAPTER SEVEN

A WEEK later I was out for a walk with Sousanna. She was explaining in lavish detail the apoplectic seizure that her soon-to-be-ex-husband had on receiving news of the Viking funeral of most of his prized possessions.

"What did he say about the car?" I asked as we passed by The Thicket, a swampy area that would have been perfect for dumping a body if it wasn't an Audubon Sanctuary and covered in snow, as it was at the moment.

She scoffed. "His lawyer said it was destruction of property, but since my name was on the registration as well...."

"You told him to suck it."

Quick nod before she sighed. "God, this weather is ridiculous."

"How so?"

"Well, in 2015 we got, what, I want to say three feet of snow around this time. Last March was balmy and warm, and this year—well, you can see. It's rainy and windy, and I bet we get more snow."

"That's Mother Nature keeping you on your toes."

"She's drunk. She needs to go home and sleep it off."

I chuckled, watching her as we walked up Wharf Street.

"What are you looking at?"

"Those are the most ridiculous snow boots I've ever seen."

"So judgmental today," she commented. "Maybe you need to get laid."

It was lucky I wasn't drinking anything or I would have choked. "I'm sorry?"

"What are you waiting for? You're gorgeous! What's your excuse?"

"What about you?" I volleyed.

"I'm sorry, I've been married for the past twenty-five years. The only one who's been out on dates is my soon-to-be ex."

I grunted.

"Laid," she said snidely. "Who am I supposed to be sleeping with?"

"Maybe the handsome man who's been lurking around your mailbox for the past two days," I suggested.

She turned to look at me. "Who?"

I shot her a look.

"You mean Dave?"

My grin, I made certain, was evil.

"Oh no," she said dismissively, smacking my arm. "He's just a friend."

"From where?"

"From college."

I nodded. "And?"

"And what?"

"Did he never marry? Have kids?"

"He did."

"If you make me dig, I'll just run home, and you'll have to walk for the next ten minutes here or so alone."

She rolled her eyes. "His son is working out there at the Marine Science Center, so he's been by a few times to see him."

"Uh-huh."

"You're being ridiculous. He's just checking on his son Kyle."

"Because Kyle is so much in need of being fussed over," I concluded.

"Dave's—"

"A very handsome man," I reminded her. "Very Sean Connery in *The Hunt For Red October*."

"Oh dear God."

"What? He is."

Her eyes darted to mine. "He's not interested in me, dear."

I was quiet as we made the left onto Nahant Road. "Because why?"

"I'm old."

"You are so not old. In what realm of the imagination is fifty-seven old?"

"Ask my ex."

"Idiots don't count."

Her laughter was good to hear. It was nice to have a friend who had no clue that I was a very bad man or that she should have been frightened of me, but who, at the same time, accepted things like people coming and going from my house at weird hours, so completely in stride.

"Don't hide behind something as asinine as a number."

We walked in silence toward Ocean Street.

"Hey, I have a question."

She regarded me warily.

"Not about your love life."

She thawed, smiling again. "Oh, then go ahead."

I snorted out a laugh. "When I'm sitting on the back porch looking out at the ocean, if I look left a little, there's an island. What is that?"

"Oh, that's Egg Rock."

"Egg Rock?"

She nodded. "It used to have a lighthouse on it, but it's been gone for a while. Only birds out there now."

"They should rebuild the lighthouse. It would be very touristy."

"Perhaps. You know, when I was learning to sail as a kid, the first solo sail was from the wharf, out around Egg Rock, and if you could do it, they gave you a T-shirt that said 'Egg Rock or Bust!'"

I just looked at her.

"What? It's a cute story."

"Mmmm," I agreed. "Hey, why aren't we walking your dogs?"

"They're napping. I'll take them out later."

"Shouldn't the dogs be on your schedule?"

She considered that a moment. "Perhaps, but I think they're holding out for you taking them on another run."

"Oh, they liked that last night, did they?" I teased.

"Are you kidding? You went for what, five miles or so? They're greyhounds, they were in heaven!"

We were all frozen by the time we got back, but the company had been good. Normally I ran alone, but she'd let Archie and Wanda out and they caught me easily, keeping pace the whole time, never once making me have to yell at them to come back or keep up. The same could not be said of all my running partners over the years.

"You know, I'm not the only one with a gentleman caller."

Her statement took me by surprise. "I'm sorry?"

"You've had that absolutely stunning man haunting your front porch since yesterday."

Stunning man? "Who?"

She waggled her eyebrows.

"You mean Mercer, who works for me?"

"No," she said, like I was deluded. "No, no, no."

"I introduced you to him."

"Yes, dear, I know, and that's not who I'm talking about."

"He's a very handsome man."

"Who, Mercer?"

"Yeah."

"If you like big and scary, then yes, probably."

I chuckled. "All right, so if you're not talking about Mercer, I'm at a loss. He's the only one who even knows where I live besides Rahm, who you met as well."

"Oh yes, Rahm," she sighed. "Now *that* is a handsome man."

"Good Lord."

"He is! He took my breath clean away."

"I guess if you go in for tall, dark, and slightly menacing."

"Which I do."

I groaned, but then it hit me. "So not Rahm, then. Someone else?"

"Yes, dear."

I was immediately worried, concerned that I'd let my guard down just in time to be murdered by whomever Trevan's boss had hired.

"Tell me what he looked like."

"Very pretty and talks to himself."

"Pardon me?"

"He has entire conversations with himself on the way to and from your front door. And while I can't hear what he's saying from my porch, I know that he asks himself questions and then answers them."

We started walking again, and then a jolt of recognition hit me.

I had been standing on the enormous wrap-around porch on the Lahm Tidewater-style home in Essex, Connecticut, watching Efrem in the backyard. His mother, Livia, walked up beside me, put her hand on my shoulder, and watched him with me.

"What is he doing?" I turned to look at the beautiful stately woman I had finally fallen in love with after many holiday visits. Efrem's father and I had bonded right away, but his mother had been unsure of me, certain that her son was in far deeper than I was. That had changed when she came to visit us in Savannah and found me nursing her son through a bout of the flu. Anyone who could still love him when he looked that disgusting, she was sure was a keeper. I'd been thrilled to have her fuss over me as well. Just because I didn't need a new mother didn't mean I didn't like the hugs and kisses and worry.

"He's working something out," she answered, returning my attention to her.

We both watched him pace, flail his arms, and talk out loud.

"Huh."

"It looks like he's nuts, right?"

"Yes," I said, chuckling.

"He's always done it, even when he was little. I was worried at first that he was talking to someone else and they were answering."

I snorted.

"But it turns out that it's just what he does."

"I wonder what he's trying to figure out."

She sighed deeply, and I turned back to her.

"I think he wants to marry you, sweetheart, and he's figuring out the pros and cons of that."

I jolted, feeling both fear and happiness slice through me at the same time. "We can't get married, he knows better. We're in the Army, for God's sake."

"I know, and I don't think he expects you both to go down to the justice of the peace, because we all know that's not even possible," she said, taking hold of my hand. "But I'm thinking he wants to ask and hear your answer, and perhaps get a promise from you and give you one in return."

I had no idea what to say.

"He loves you, his father loves you, his sisters love you, I love you, even his brother loves you; it's inevitable that he'd get to this place after five years."

I crossed my arms and took a breath.

"Don't you think so?"

"Yes."

"Aren't you in the same place?"

I nodded.

"Well, then, what do you think you'll say to my son?"

My sigh was long. "If he asks, there's only one way to answer."

She patted my shoulder. "I thought so."

That night, after his parents turned in, I went outside to look at the stars in the crisp fall air, loving November in New England and realizing that I looked forward to the holidays again, especially Thanksgiving, because of Efrem and his family.

"What are you doing out here?"

Turning, leaning against the porch railing, I regarded the beautiful man who I fell more in love with every day. It was sappy but true. When he squinted at me, like usual, like clockwork, without even making a conscious choice, I was charmed. It turned out that everything Efrem Lahm did melted me right to the floor. It didn't hurt that he was drop-dead gorgeous. But I realized that more than anything, his smooth whiskey voice with just a trace of gravel did all kinds of wicked and wild things to my libido. The man was irresistible, and I wasn't the only one who thought so.

"What are you thinking?"

I shook my head.

"No, come on," he prodded, moving forward, walking in and out of the shadows as he crossed the porch to me.

"Last weekend when we were at that fall festival downtown, I was waiting for you to bring food to the table, and while I was sitting there, holding our spot, I saw you walking back and realized that I wasn't the only one looking at you."

"I see," he said, distracted, reaching me and putting his hands on my hips as he stepped in close, trailing his lips over the underside of my jaw.

From my vantage point, I'd been able to see all the men and women caught in my lover's wake. All ages and flavors responded to the sleek muscles on his broad-shouldered, narrow-waisted frame and the long, toned legs encased in faded denim moving him in a fluid, swaggering stride down the street. His walk was enticing, as was the siren call of the slow, sexy smile he bestowed like a blessing. It was amazing—even though it was never his intention to be magnetic and seductive, between the sinful curl of his lips and how intent he was when he gave you all his attention, people swarmed him like bees on honeycomb. I'd found myself sighing just as I was doing now through the kisses that reached my mouth.

Taking his face in my hands, I tipped his head back and turned a sweet kiss into a serious one that had him whimpering in seconds. Pulling back, I stared down into his gorgeous eyes, the blown pupils making me smile.

"You know, just your breath on my skin drives me crazy," he rasped, nibbling along my jaw. "The kissing is just overkill."

I chuckled. "I'll remember that."

He cleared his throat. "I want you to marry me."

If his mother hadn't warned me, I'd have been shocked speechless. Instead… "Why's that?"

His brows furrowed, and I tried not to laugh.

"The hell kind of a question is that?" He was indignant.

I tried to get myself under control, but he looked so put out. "Honey—"

"Why the *hell* do you think I want to marry you?"

"Baby—"

"You're such an ass! This is my goddamn romantic gesture."

I lunged at him, grabbing him fast, and when I lifted him off his feet, he did what was normal and expected and wrapped those strong legs around my hips tight. "Ask me again. Please."

Shaky breath in. "Marry me."

"Love to."

"Yes? Was that a yes?"

"That was a yes."

He kissed me to seal the deal, going slow, licking over my lower lip before taking my mouth. When he eased back just enough to whisper, I struggled to hear him over the pounding of my heart.

"As soon as we're out, wherever we are, we find a way to tie to the knot. Promise me. No matter what time it is, early in the morning, late in the afternoon, no matter where in the world we are, we figure it out so we'll be husband and husband. I need it. I want it—so swear."

"I do," I vowed before I kissed him again.

"Oh," she chirped happily, returning me to the present. "You know who it is."

"I might," I said softly. "Pretty, you said?"

"I did," Sousanna assured me.

"How pretty?"

"Very."

"Blond?"

"Yes."

"Could you see dimples?"

"I could, yes."

What the hell was Efrem Lahm doing on Nahant? And how? No records placed me there, and my dummy corporation purchased the house—no way could someone follow that back to me. It was impossible, even with the top security clearance I used to have. So if Efrem really was there, I had two questions: how and why? But more than that, after our last exchange, why would he even bother making the trip? We both knew he had an agenda. He wanted to know my secrets, and it wasn't going to happen. I would never let him make a fool out of me again. Once was more than enough... if he truly had. To say I doubted my own conclusions was an understatement, but to say I was questioning the conclusion I came to in the first place—I was not. It came down a simple question: Could I trust Efrem Lahm?

The answer was a resounding no.

Could I say conclusively that he was after answers about *who I was* and not *where I'd been*? No, I could not. The problem was that it was possible—and just as likely as the opposite scenario. But what was the point of even figuring it out? The time for Efrem and me had long since passed. It was better to let the very idea of a happily-ever-after go before I made myself crazy with possibilities.

What it all boiled down to was that it was impossible for either of us to trust the other. I couldn't possibly hope to know what his true intentions were, and mine were just as blurry to him. There was really no way to be a hundred percent sure of where we each stood, and because of who we were and what we did for a living, uncertainty could get us killed. I wasn't about to risk not only myself but everyone who depended on me, and so had settled it all in my head logically and cast out all thought of Efrem... until I thought about him again.

"Darius, you look like you're in pain," Sousanna remarked. "Are you all right?"

"I'm not sure yet."

"Do you want to talk about him?"

"Who?" I asked, turning to her.

"The man with the dimples."

"Not at the moment, no."

"Maybe later? We could have tea," she said, slipping her arm into the curve of mine.

"I hate tea," I grumbled, appreciating her trying to comfort me.

"Oh, you do not," she said, laughing softly and patting my arm.

We walked on, parting before we reached our respective houses, not quite to the end of Ocean Street, before the park, but close.

"So I was right. I *am* the talk of Dunkin' Donuts," she called over to me before she disappeared inside her house.

"You're not supposed to be proud of that," I called back before I recognized a dangerous man on the beach side of the street, leaning on the hood of his car, managing to look both bored and irritated at the same time.

It was fast, the punch of adrenaline, the one that had kept me alive for years, my senses faster than others because I'd been taught not to filter. It wasn't, *Oh, something's wrong, out of sequence, out of place*, it was simply *danger*, and then the gun was being unloaded. So instead of my brain figuring out friend or foe, I went immediately on the offensive.

But then I stopped and really looked at him and took a breath. Yet another reason I was glad to retire, my reflexes were quickly deteriorating under a sea of friendship.

Normally, just because I was who I was—even though the man wasn't looking at me with deadly intent—I still would have lowered the zipper on my shearling-lined brown leather jacket and reached inside for my gun. But I didn't because really, I knew him, and if he was going to go against Ceaton's orders for some reason and kill me, he could have done it already.

"Hey," I called over instead of the million other things I could have done just a half a year ago.

Marko Borodin gave me a head tip but made no other move.

"What are you doing here?" I asked, not nervous—it would take a lot more than Borodin to do that—but cautious. I'd checked him out, as I had all the men on Ceaton's team, and while the others had only ever worked for Grigor Jankovic, Borodin was ex-Spetsnaz, Russian Special Forces and had been with the Federal Security Service of the Russian Federation before leaving his homeland. After that, once he was stateside, I'd found no record of him at all. He'd come in on a tourist visa that expired and no one ever followed up even though no records showed him ever leaving the country. Three years later, he'd become a naturalized citizen. It was amazing to me that, with his record, Borodin had been able to get first a green card and then actual citizen status, but with enough money changing hands, I knew anything was possible. What was more interesting to me was that he suddenly turned up in Las Vegas, working for a man named Bohdan. I had no idea how a highly decorated major in the Russian Army ended up working for a Serbian mob boss, but I hadn't looked any further into it. I trusted Ceaton, and if he vouched for Borodin, I had nothing to say.

Still, it was disconcerting to see him without his boss, but I could certainly handle him if something was awry.

"Your neighbor, the woman, she has contract out on her," he explained with a yawn. "I told... Farmer, Farney, Farrington—"

"Farley," I volunteered, knowing who he meant.

"*Da*," he agreed, giving me a slight grin. "I told him, I would not interfere with his work, but I must protect my interests."

"Meaning me."

He nodded.

"I appreciate that."

"But then Ceaton reminds me, your neighbors on both sides are off-limits."

"Yes."

"So Farley is in trunk, and I am waiting to speak to you."

He'd been in no hurry, content to let Farley get frostbite. "Nice of you," I sighed, trotting across the street to him. Together, we walked around the back of the Mercedes sedan, and Marko popped the trunk for me.

Lying on his side with his wrists and ankles and mouth duct-taped was twenty-six-year-old Castor Farley, a new up-and-coming contract killer out of Long Beach who was making a name for himself by killing wives, husbands, mistresses, and boytoys of rich men. People let him get close—too close, obviously—because he looked like a chilled-out surfer until the moment he pulled out his gun and shot them in the head.

As soon as he saw me, his turquoise eyes got huge, and he started shaking.

"Just wait," I told him, lifting my hand.

His eyes darted to Marko, who was screwing a suppressor onto his gun, which didn't help his panic in any way.

"What is that?" I asked, distracted, because it was a nice-looking pistol.

He palmed it, letting me have a look. "Is Heckler and Koch 23."

I took it from him, testing the weight, did a clearance check, and lifted it, aimed, and then passed it back. "It's nice."

He shrugged. "I am trying out new things."

I smiled at him and then looked back down at Farley, who looked like he was about ready to pass out. "I live next door," I told him.

The shaking got worse then.

Marko turned his head to look at me. "All this talking is too much. I found place by docks that turns him into fish food for small fee. I will go now," he finished, reaching up to close the trunk.

I lifted my hand, and his frustrated sigh was actually funny. "You in a hurry?" I asked.

"You and Ceaton, always so much explaining," he said, his voice full of disgust. "Better to just use gun."

This was why Ceaton was in charge. I turned back to the man in the trunk. "Listen," I said to Farley. "Stay out of Boston, all right?"

He nodded vigorously.

"Who put out the contract?" I asked. "The husband?"

Second nod.

"Put the word out: she's off-limits as a favor to me."

He said something into the tape.

I tipped my head at Marko, and he removed it fast. It hurt like hell—I knew from experience—Farley's wide, supple mouth was now covered in angry red welts.

"What?" I asked.

"I will stay out of Boston. You don't have to tell me twice."

I grunted.

"Please," he begged. "I swear to you."

"People will say you are going soft," Marko assured me. "Let me take care of this."

"Harris!" Farley gasped.

I shook my head at Marko. "We'll give him one chance."

He yawned. "Is your business, not mine, but so we are clear, if I see him again, I can kill him, *da*? We are agreed?"

"Yes."

He grunted before pulling a butterfly knife from inside his coat and cutting the tape off Farley's wrists and ankles. "Get out of my car."

Farley scrambled fast.

"Thank you," I said to Marko.

"*Nye zaboyteya*," he mumbled, moving toward the driver's side door.

"Hey."

He turned back to look at me.

"Somebody here in Nahant will make people into fish food?" That surprised me more than anything else, even the contract on my friend.

"In Boston," he clarified. "I would never dispose of body this close to your home."

"That's very considerate, thank you."

"Freeze!"

We all turned to find *my ex*—the guy who could make my stomach flip just by being near me—braced for battle in the middle of the street, holding a gun on all three of us.

"What are you doing here?" I asked, angrier than I thought I'd be. He had no right to be in my new life when he was squarely part of the old. It wasn't fair. I didn't want him there reminding me of things I couldn't have.

His head lifted slowly. "Are you all right?" he asked Farley.

"Yeah, man, I'm fine. Who the fuck are you?" Farley groused.

Efrem lowered his arm, holding the gun at his side. "You're pissed at me? I'm saving your life!"

"Nah, man, Harris saved my life," Farley retorted. "And I don't wanna get caught in the middle when Ivan Drago here shoots your ass."

"Ivan Drago," Marko growled drolly. "I have never heard this before."

"It's a film reference from—"

"Run now," I suggested to Farley since, clearly, he'd missed class the day they taught sarcasm.

Farley was not stupid. He turned and bolted.

"Darius!"

We all turned again, this time toward Sousanna's front door, which was just across her manicured front lawn.

"What do you want?" I barked, not wanting her to get hurt but more than that, not wanting her to see Efrem since he wasn't going to be staying.

"To make sure you're all right!" she shouted back. "But now I don't care!"

I grinned at her, and she smiled back before pointing at Efrem.

"That's the pretty one, by the way."

"I figured," I told her and then pointed at Marko. "This is another associate of mine, Marko Borodin. You'll see him around with Ceaton."

"Oh, lovely," she said, beaming now. Clearly she liked the looks of the much deadlier and ten times more terrifying Russian over Ceaton Mercer. "Would any of you like some tea?"

"No—"

"*Da,*" Marko called out quickly and started toward her house.

I stared after him a moment, stunned, and when I switched and gave her my attention, I noted how excited she seemed, bouncing on her toes, holding the door, her attention fully focused on Marko and none on me or Efrem.

She shook his hand when he reached the porch and then slipped her arm through the crook of his before they went inside.

Everyone in my life was insane.

"The hell is that?" I muttered a second before Efrem stepped into my line of vision.

"What in the world is—"

I gestured at the house, lost in the idea that my sweet next-door neighbor was having tea with a man who could kill her and stuff her down her garbage disposal without even a rise in his blood pressure. And if not for me, they would have never been in each another's orbit. The responsibility was staggering, and nobody but me knew that. To them, it was tea. "Ceaton's scary, but Marko isn't? Seriously? Is she deluded?" I asked Efrem.

Efrem looked over his shoulder at her home and then back at me as a car pulled up in front of my house. "I have no idea what you're— could you please just focus on—"

"Now what are you doing here?" I asked out loud as Lee got out of a sleek sports car. "I just saw you," I complained.

The day I was having, Jesus Christ. It was too many things all at once, past and present, crashing down on me, and I was feeling ungrounded.

"Yes, I know," he said, smirking at me as he crossed the street without checking for traffic, the swagger on full display.

I gestured at the car. "What is that?"

He rolled his eyes. "That is a Maserati GranTurismo MC Centennial Coupe."

"You rented that?"

Instant scowl. "Why would I rent that?" he asked disdainfully.

"That's my question."

His top lip curled up in distaste. "I bought it," he said dryly.

"So that's yours."

He grunted.

"Then why is it here? You don't live here, you live in Seoul and Manhattan and—"

"I know where I live," he assured me.

"What's the car doing here?"

"I need it to drive around in. I can't just fly a plane to get around in the city."

A thought hit me. "Tell me you're not loading and unloading that car onto the plane."

He waggled his eyebrows.

"When did I say you could do that?" I yelled at him. There was no doubt in my mind that the people who had asked me to assume the role of the vault were already sorry they'd picked me. The people I'd chosen—this one in particular—was far too high-maintenance and more importantly, high profile. "We're supposed to fly under the radar!"

He drew so much attention to himself, and I realized that what I was feeling was worry.

"Goddammit!" I was becoming ridiculously sentimental, and that had never happened before I'd become the vault, before Ceaton, before... before me wanting a *change*. And now I was also going to fuss over Lee like a big brother. Just thinking about it was horrifying.

"Aish," he muttered, making a face, waving his hand dismissively like I was just too annoying to deal with. "Just go inside and pack, or we can buy you new clothes when we get there, which I would prefer."

"I'm sorry, what?" I didn't even sound upset, I sounded pained, because I couldn't just shoot him anymore—he was part of my team, and I cared about him just like I did Ceaton and Trevan and Rahm Daoud and Christopher Mancuso and Duncan Stiel and... fuck, *where did it end*? When did becoming the vault become me protecting people? I didn't want to be counted on or trusted or... it was spiraling out of control.

"What?" Lee asked irritably.

"Why do I have to buy clothes?"

He indicated me with another flourish of his hand. "You dress terribly."

"Says the man wearing… what are you wearing?"

"An overcoat and a suit and a turtleneck," he told me, speaking slowly, the condescension crystal clear in his voice.

But when he said it, it sounded like nothing, like he wasn't wearing three shades of blue with skinny pants and leather loafers. He should have been on the cover of a fashion magazine. Normal people didn't dress like that.

"I look fine, thank you." I grumbled at him.

His grunt was not convincing.

"Why are you here?" I almost whined.

"You need to come to Dubai with me."

Efrem moved to stand at my shoulder, and I felt his hand slip to the middle of my back. It was instinctive, possessive, and while I felt the throb of excitement make my stomach flutter, I reminded myself that he was not for me and leaned away from him.

He took a step closer, crowding me, shifting, pressing into my space, and this time I took several steps away.

"What are you doing?" he asked sharply.

"I think the more important question is *what* are *you* doing?" I volleyed, rounding on Efrem, standing beside Lee.

He gestured at me. "I want to talk to you."

"We have nothing to talk about. You should go home."

"Nothing to talk about? Are you insane?"

"I get the feeling I might be interrupting something," Lee said, turning his head to look at me.

"You're not. He was just leaving."

"The hell I am," Efrem insisted, rounding on Lee. "And why the hell are you going to Dubai, and who are you to Darius?"

"Who?" Lee asked him, squinting.

He pointed at me.

"Harris, you mean?"

"Darius Hawthorne," Efrem explained.

Lee pivoted to me. "How many names do you have?"

"Three, but Darius is the real one."

"Interesting. Did you use Harris for your business because it's the one you used before?"

"Yes."

He nodded. "That makes sense. What do you want me to use?"

God. "Darius," I sighed, tired already and it wasn't even lunchtime yet.

His smile was sinister and smug at the same time. "Does Homeland here know all about you? Yes or no?"

"No," I told him.

"Does he know what you do?"

"No, but he'd like to," I said, my eyes flicking to Efrem. "That's why he's here."

"That's a lie," Efrem said flatly. "I don't care at all what you do. I just want to know where you've been so I can figure out my next step."

"You have no next step."

"Oh, I think I do."

Lee faced Efrem. "So, you want to do what, find out all his secrets? Penetrate his defenses?"

"It's not like that at all."

"But he won't tell you, will he? He's like a grape on a plate that you're trying to stab with a fork, but no matter how hard you try to pin him down, spear him, he keeps bouncing and rolling away." Lee tsked. "Perhaps you should try another tactic."

I looked at him. "What the hell was that?"

He appeared confused. "A metaphor. Clearly."

I pointed several feet away. "Go stand there." He rolled his eyes but moved, and I rounded on Efrem. "You need to leave."

"Darius, I—"

"You need to go," I demanded icily. "Build your case some other way than on the bones of our dead relationship."

He looked like I hit him, he squinted, but I saw the welling tears anyway, saw the wobble of his chin, the clench of his jaw, and heard the sharp indrawn breath. If I'd hit him, it would have hurt less, that was clear.

"Dead?" he whispered. "I've been holding on for dear life for seventeen years, and you're telling me 'us' is already dead?"

After so long, after so many deaths, so much blood, pain, and heartache, this—Efrem coming apart in front of me—this was what was going to break me down.

"You never thought about me?"

I swallowed so I wouldn't speak.

"I searched so hard for you that I was still a captain by the time I got out."

Wow. Still a captain after that long. He must have been passed over for promotion at least twice. He hadn't been a total fuckup, they hadn't kicked him out—but they must have quietly separated him.

"I have the bare minimum of security clearance because whatever I'm given, I've used to search for you."

I remembered his voice when he was hurting, and this was what it sounded like, soft, crackly, the hitches of breath and the raw, dark look in his eyes. If this was an act, he was missing his calling, and moving to Hollywood should have been a priority.

"No private detective I've ever hired could find anything about you. I got a lead a few years ago because I found your friend Detective Stiel, and when I showed him your picture, he said your name was Terrence Moss but he had no idea where you were either."

The urge to touch him was almost unbearable and watching him break down was torture because I loved him, plain and simple, always had, always would. Even after his betrayal in Detroit—or what I was almost certain was one—it didn't change that, just my plans for my future. But now he was right here in front of me explaining that he'd never, ever stopped trying to find me.

Maybe, just possibly, I'd misread things—not that it mattered… but still….

"You looked for me?"

"Of course," he rasped, his voice cracking. "How could I not?"

It was a jumble in my head, what I wanted and what seemed possible were so far apart and, because it was Efrem, I was off balance. Because when you were in love, that's what you were—

tipped sideways, your feet not quite touching the ground. It was what love did: turned you upside-down.

Fuck.

"You're a Homeland Security agent," I said, taking a step toward him instead of away. "You know that you being here is—"

"When did you stop loving me?" he asked, and I heard how broken his voice was, saw how lost he looked, like I'd ripped away his anchor line and left him adrift. "Just so I can know how long I've been walking around without it."

"I used to be so control of my life," I murmured before I rushed him and wrapped him up in my arms.

He didn't hug me back, just stood there and shuddered, like he was going to fly apart.

People complicated everything. When it was just me, alone, I would have never cared about Marko turning a guy into fish food or if Landry's shop was close to Trevan's restaurant or if Lee wasn't being careful with flying his car all over the world or if Mancuso shot Daoud or the other way around. I would not have saved Ceaton, would not have checked up on Duncan many times over the years, or made certain that my sweet next-door neighbor didn't die and make her dogs orphans. I'd let people near me who cluttered up my life with... well, life. I hadn't been living in so long that I forgot what it was like to be responsible to, and for, others.

"Bored," Lee announced from behind me.

I groaned, and Efrem caught his breath and nuzzled his face into the hollow of my throat.

"You know it's a lie," I told him.

"What part?" He inhaled deeply, stopped leaning on me, and lifted his arms to coil them around my waist.

"You know I could never stop loving you. It's permanent, has been since the night we walked home together from the bar that time."

"For me it was the first time I saw you. I felt like I was hit by a lightning bolt. I knew I'd never be the same."

I closed my eyes as his arms tightened, and he pressed tight against me, shivering from the contact, not the cold. I knew him; he'd been raised in Connecticut, the man would have done well in Siberia, he was so immune to Arctic temperatures. So it could only be one thing, and that was me. *I* was making him tremble.

"I would never, could never, do anything to hurt you in any way," he said gruffly between sniffles. "I've lived all this time, had a career, friends, family, possessions, all of it, everything you're supposed to have for a happy life, and it's been nice, it's been fine, but I haven't been happy or present or even really living since you've been gone."

I was the exact same. I'd swaddled myself first in missions and a life of service to my country, and then to the dollar, and then to the challenge of the untouchable mark that I'd never failed to achieve, and finally was handed a position only a handful of people would ever even know existed, but still I walked around feeling like I'd left the iron on at home. Like I was missing something, like I'd forgotten to do something, and my world could implode at any moment.

Of course it was Efrem.

He was my other half, made for me, and living without him, once my life was no longer a series of split-second choices, was never a viable solution. When you were moving at the speed of sound, being alone made sense, but as soon as the scenery outside the window became recognizable shapes instead of a steady blur, you longed for home. Efrem was the only home I had, and the constant ache in my chest was the yearning for him. It was kind of late in the day to have my epiphany, but as I clutched at the man I loved, I was thankful to have it at all.

"I'm only me," he whispered, "and did I fuck up? Yeah, I fucked up. I shouldn't have taken you back to the office. I should have driven you somewhere secluded and told you that I love—I love you, and that I can't—I *won't* be away from you even one more second. I don't care what has to happen, just let me keep you and my family. That's all that matters."

"Everything else is expendable, huh?" I asked, rubbing my face in his hair, letting the warmth of his body seep into mine.

"Yes."

"Your career?"

"Yes."

"Friends, colleagues, you don't care what they think?"

"No, I don't care."

"You have an important job."

"That a hundred people could do better."

I doubted that, but like me, distracted, we weren't on top of our game.

"I really do have other things to do besides watch you maul your man," Lee complained, sounding ten kinds of surly.

The "your man" was nice, though, and so I let Efrem go and turned to look at Lee.

"Yeah?" he asked, eyebrows lifted, appearing hopeful.

I gestured for him, and he charged back over.

"Why?" I asked Lee.

"Why what?"

I just stared at him.

"Why Dubai, you mean."

"Yes," I said as Efrem pressed against my side again, fitting like he always had, under my arm, his around my back, his left hand splayed over my abdomen.

"Am I talking in front of Homeland?" Lee asked, tipping his head at Efrem.

"Yeah, go ahead," I replied and heard Efrem take a breath because just the simple words put us on solid footing. Yes, I needed to talk to him, and yes, we had to figure out everything that had gone on in that office between my paranoia and his need to know—wires may have gotten crossed or, more likely, tangled up in a snarl of uncertainty.

"There's an issue with a sheikh who wants us to take in his daughter."

I sighed. I was going to have to go. The vault was always the one who took in people. "And?"

"And he doesn't want her falling into the hands of anyone who would use her as leverage against him, but more importantly, he wants her to be a doctor and not an ornament."

"So he needs her to disappear."

"For a time, yes, until this one particular man—" He stopped suddenly and grinned at me, just in case I missed it, just in case I wasn't smart enough to follow his clever subtext, "—is no longer in power."

He was ridiculously transparent. "You want to kill this guy instead of taking in the girl."

"I do."

Of course he did, any chance to kill someone and he was happy. "Tell me about the would-be groom."

"Weapons dealer, guns, gas, you name it, he's got it."

"Selling them to?"

"Very disreputable men," he finished with a wink.

"Well then."

"But then we get what from the girl's father for doing him this service?" Lee asked.

"I'm sure that if I need him to house anything we find can't be easily disposed of once we raid this man's weapon stores, that he'll be more than willing to help us out."

He nodded.

"Broker that deal, and if you have any trouble, I'll get on a plane."

"I'll send *my* plane for you," he informed me.

Which was really *my* plane, but whatever. "Fine."

Lee turned to leave, but I reached out and grabbed his shoulder. "Did you get rid of that gun I gave you last week?"

"The one your friend gave you to get rid of?"

Talking to him was going to give me hives. "How many guns have I given you?"

He had to think. "Three. No, four. No, yes, three."

"You're exhausting," I said tiredly. I really needed to be alone with Efrem, and the thought crossed my mind that if I just shot Lee, I'd at least have that faster. Making him my bishop may have been an overly hasty decision.

Quick flashing grin, just to be annoying, "So I've been told."

"What was I thinking?"

"I still have no earthly idea."

"Who are you?" Efrem asked, and Lee looked at him.

"We met last time," Lee reminded him. "Did you forget already? How old are you?"

Efrem stepped away from me and crossed his arms, scowling. "What?"

"I get that your world is scary, so how has he not been shot?"

"This is an excellent question," I said, chuckling, taking a breath, letting the tension roll out of me. "Come inside," I invited Efrem before turning toward the house.

"Am I leaving now, or am I coming inside too?" Lee asked cheekily.

"Go," I ordered, not turning around, on a mission now to get inside and warm and get Efrem Lahm talking and then, hopefully, God willing, into my bed.

"Did I see Farley earlier?" Lee called over to me.

"Don't kill Farley," I insisted, hearing how belligerent I sounded as Efrem moved up beside me, following closely, then slipping his hand into mine.

"He didn't take the contract out on you, did he?"

Efrem sucked in a breath beside me.

"No, he was after my neighbor."

"I didn't think he did. That would have been ballsy, and Farley doesn't strike me as particularly brave."

"That contract is dead. There's nobody worth worrying about who will take it."

"You talked to Daoud?"

"I did."

"And Mancuso?"

"And Mancuso!"

"Besides me, that's everybody."

"You forgot Isaak."

Even from how far away I was now, I heard the disgusted scoff behind me. "That fat fuck Russian, he'll get it in some brothel, mark my words."

I didn't care enough to find out what Lee had against Isaak Skriabin. "Consider the contract closed."

"You want me to take out Eastman?"

"No," I said irritably, stopping and turning around to look at him. "Just do your job."

"Fine. But if I see Farley after this, can I kill him?"

"No. Marko has dibs."

"Who?"

I growled at Lee, which Efrem smiled over. Apparently I was appealing while all petulant and gruff. "I told you about—"

"Oh yes, yes, Mercer's guy," Lee answered as he opened the car door.

"Yeah, so—"

"No, that's fine."

"What's fine?"

"I read Marko's bio," he said happily. "From everything I saw, him killing Farley would be excruciating. I'm good to watch."

"What did Farley ever do to you?"

"He blew up a yacht I was on."

I stared at him.

He stared back.

"A yacht?" Efrem asked into the void of sound, squeezing my hand still in his. "That you were *on*?"

Lee made a noise in the back of his throat. "It was a big yacht, and the end I was on didn't detonate, merely sank, but still... he was responsible, and there was nothing out there but a lot of water and a million sharks."

"And yet," I said, gesturing at him.

"I didn't say I was without a backup plan, but that was hardly the point."

"You and Farley are not on equal playing fields. Cut the man some slack."

He winced.

"Please."

"Fine," he begrudgingly agreed.

"Call me if you need me."

He rolled his eyes. "Like I need you to kill people."

I pivoted and headed for the path leading to my front door.

"He's just going to—and you just ordered him to—"

"I did," I said, yanking him after me, jogging now toward the front door.

"Why are you hurrying?" he asked softly. "Not that I'm complaining."

"God only knows who else will show up."

He followed along, no plea to stop, no order to slow down, not even a gentle request to let him think for a second. There was only him keeping up.

Chapter Eight

ONCE WE were inside, I slammed the door closed behind me and locked it before rounding on him. I wasn't sure whether I wanted to yell at him or kiss him.

"Are you going to take my coat?"

Shit. Leave it to Efrem to make with the niceties.

I gestured at the couch. "Just throw it over there."

He took it off and draped it over the closest high-backed leather chair instead. It was a good chair, done in that quilted style. The whole room was done in complementary shades of brown that made it warm, even in a big space.

The moment we were both without our cold-weather gear, he crossed his arms and faced me, looking both contrite and pissed off at the same time.

"I want to hear the story from the last time I saw you," he demanded, glaring at me.

"You tell me about this turnaround first."

The scowl furrowed his brows. "There's no turnaround, you misread the situation entirely, and you know it."

"I'm sorry?"

"Don't deflect," he warned me, taking a step closer. "You thought something horrible, and you need to apologize."

I crossed my arms. "It looked bad."

"The point is that you misjudged me, and you know better."

My eyes searched his.

"Apologize."

"Why were you pushing?"

"Because I wanted to know where the hell you'd been for so long."

"You came off more rendition than reunion."

He smirked. "Is that supposed to be clever?"

"You had an agenda in that room."

He nodded. "I have no idea what happened to you, but did I think that maybe if I got you to tell me everything that you could be safe and be back to being mine—there is that possibility."

"So you admit that you were pushing, and not just out of personal interest."

"It was *all* personal," he informed me. "It's only *ever* been that."

I stared at him, weighing the past and the present and every little thing I knew about Efrem Lahm.

"There's no one who knows me better than you."

I was thinking the same thing.

"And you forgot that while we were in that room together."

It was true.

"I've thought about our conversation over and over, replayed it in my head a million times at this point, and I'll give you that, somewhere in the middle, it went from just wanting to know about you to wanting to know where the bodies are buried."

I could not stop staring at his eyes, the way they caught the light, the blue in the depths of the green that you didn't notice unless you were close. Most people thought Efrem's eyes were pale green—even up close that could be the case—but with me they always darkened almost immediately. His mother had noticed the very first Christmas we visited her, the first winter after we met.

"Oh, well now," she said, smiling at me. "I thought only his father's eyes did that, but apparently my son sees something he likes."

I turned in question.

"My husband's eyes got dark like that the first time he saw me," she said, nudging my side with her elbow. It was adorable, and I'd been under her spell almost instantly. What she was telling me was important. Efrem's eyes got deep and dark when he was looking at me, as they were now, as they'd been that day in the interrogation room. He couldn't fake that honesty.

"Shit."

He grunted smugly.

"We were both ridiculous."

"Yes."

"I doubted you and then my instincts kicked in."

"And I was so involved in wanting to know everything that I lost sight of the fact that I had you right there in front of me."

I took a breath. "It was painful to think that all I was, was a means to an end to you."

"It gutted me to see the look on your face—like I betrayed you after all that time."

We were silent, staring at each other.

"I'm sorry," I whispered.

"So am I."

We stood there and I noticed, as I always had, how really beautiful he was. The indigo chips in his deep green eyes framed by long, golden lashes were as stunning as ever. Red rimmed at the moment from welling tears—that was my doing.

"I wonder what you would have done if our roles were reversed in that interrogation room."

"Hopefully," he said hoarsely, "had more faith."

"I would have pushed just as hard," I admitted, putting myself in his shoes.

"Yes, but you were always better under pressure." He sighed. "You would have found a way not to become unhinged."

"Is that what you were?"

"Well, obviously," he muttered, clearly wrung out. "You were suddenly there and I had so many different emotions running through my head that I got completely overwhelmed."

And I had read that as desperation to get answers for Homeland, not merely as him wanting to find out about me—which was wrong.

"Were you so unaffected that you kept your wits about you the whole time?"

"Clearly not."

He turned away from me, head down, and I was close enough to hear his staccato breathing as though he were verging on crying.

"I misread things," I husked out, stepping in beside him.

"I wasn't helping, but as I said, I was a bit distraught," he choked out. "I mean, I knew I made a mess of things, and when I told my mother—"

"Your mother?"

He closed his eyes, swallowing hard. "I called her and told her I'd found you, and she was ecstatic, and so was my father—especially my father, and you'd think it would be the other way around, but he knows what it's like to live without love and then get it back and—"

My hand between his shoulder blades interrupted him and when I started rubbing slow circles, he swallowed down a sob.

"I've been paranoid a long time," I confessed, leaning in, pressing a light kiss to the side of his neck at the same time that the birds that had been fluttering around in my chest became California condors with enormous flapping wings. I could not remember ever being so nervous. The barest whisper in my brain that he could walk out the door if we didn't fix things between us had me terrified like I hadn't been in years.

He couldn't leave. I was never letting him leave.

"Which has kept you safe, I'm sure," he mumbled, returning my attention to him.

"What?"

"Being paranoid," he reminded me. "That has kept you safe."

"Yes, it has," I agreed, moving around behind him, leaning into him, my chest resting against his back, my groin at the curve of his ass.

"Well, I'm glad for that," he rasped, his voice shaking, "but again, the only thing I was looking to do that day was use whatever power I had to get close to you for purely personal reasons."

"Could you turn around and look at me?"

"I'm torn."

"In what way?" I asked, my attention captured by the highlights in his gold hair, by the strands of white and wheat, of ash blond and even some brown. It had darkened over the years but was still thick, tapering to the nape of his neck.

"Half of me wants to yell at you because you didn't have any faith in me, and that's a poor foundation to start from."

It was, he was right, but I'd changed my mind after seeing the genuine hurt in his face, in his eyes, and hearing the sincerity of his words. I could be fooled just like everyone else, but of the things I knew, the one I knew best was Efrem, and so I had to trust in him, have faith in him, and that canceled out training and habits and fear.

"And the other half of you?" I murmured, slipping my hand around his throat and tipping his head back on my shoulder.

He shuddered.

"Ef?"

His eyes were closed, and he was breathing heavy, just standing there soaking up the contact exactly like me.

"The other ha-half," he stuttered, swallowing fast, wetting his lips, a movement that had me riveted, "doesn't care about blame or anger or anything else but just getting back to where we were sixteen years ago so I can get laid."

I chuckled, and he gasped as I turned him in my arms to face me.

"You know," he said, meeting my gaze. "You think it would be such a coup to bring you in and have you spill secrets, but would they even let you?"

"What do you mean?"

"Don't get me wrong, I'm sure we all want to know where Hoffa is buried, but—"

"Now wait—"

He snorted, relaxing just a bit. "But really, things you know, that's above my paygrade, right? Above probably my boss's, so—would they, the agency, have even let you spill your secrets to me?"

I thought a moment. "You know I don't know the answer to that."

He nodded, studying my face.

Another aspect I had not considered at the time, so overwhelmed by his presence.

"You know I used to think, God, will you look at this man, what the hell is he doing with me?"

"You've got that—"

But his hand on my cheek stopped me, and on instinct, I turned my face and kissed his palm. I'd done it a thousand times, and after the smile I got, I hoped to do it a thousand more.

"I bet it's hard for you to come and go like the wind with people staring at you all the time thinking that they've never seen such a beautiful man."

"Hardly," I mumbled, having trouble thinking with his besotted gaze on me again. I had so missed seeing his face, the love in it.

His thumb slipped across my lips once, then again, and I saw him roll his shoulders, shift his stance like he was uncomfortable or his clothes were suddenly too tight, just like mine.

"I've ne-nev—never had a reaction to anyone like I do to you."

"Same," I confessed, bumping him back against the wall, my thigh slipping between his that he parted for me.

His eyes closed like they did when he was concentrating, and when I touched my forehead to his, us just standing there, breathing together, breathing each other's air, he calmed and so did I. It was natural, us, like two parts of one thing, and I felt the birds in my chest settle, roost, and the familiar ache of wanting washed through me.

It was not only his beauty that did it, or being close to him, or knowing that if I reached for him he'd come into my arms, my bed, my life—it was more than all of that. It was the overwhelming sense of peace and home that filled all the cold empty places inside that just standing in his space did to me.

He would have never hurt me. I'd made a mistake. "I really am sorry," I rumbled, the words sliding out of my throat, the regret there in my voice.

He nodded, just barely. "Me too."

"Thank you for taking a chance and coming here, I'm very happy to see you."

I was happily startled to see the scowl when I lifted my head, because it was so dear, so remembered, that my heart hurt.

"How did you find me?" I asked, letting my hands that had been settled on his hips fall away and take several steps back giving both him, and myself, room to breathe.

"I followed your friend Trevan. You don't exist. Even your file that I saw now suddenly is no longer available, and your military file is above my boss's paygrade."

"Yes."

"How did you erase your civilian file?"

"I didn't do anything, but I have people who look out for me and make certain that I don't exist on paper. It's a lot of cloak-and-dagger bullshit."

He nodded.

"So you followed Trevan?"

"Yes," he said, taking a step closer, looking me over. "Him, I can find. You just have to know what people to look for."

"Like?"

"Like him and Ceaton Mercer and Brinley Todd, the marine biologist that he lives with right here in Nahant."

"Imagine that."

"And Darius Hawthorne, who nobody used to know but me, who now owns this house."

"It's a nice house."

"It is," he agreed, stalking closer, within arm's reach of me. "It's quite cozy in here for such a big space."

My pulse was starting to race as I watched his eyes narrow, the drugged, languid quality of his movements and the weight of his stare prickling my desire for him.

"I have something to say."

"Go ahead."

"For how I handled things in the interrogation room at the Homeland Security Office," he said quickly, chin up, "I've been placed on administrative leave."

"Why?"

"Because I didn't record even a second of our conversation and didn't find out any more about Thiago Fanton's gun trafficking business than when I went in there."

"I'm sorry."

"It's not for you to be sorry about. It was my decision."

"Yeah, but—"

"I had you right there for the first time in sixteen years. I sure as hell wasn't going to waste even a second of my time talking about Fanton beyond the obvious."

I was quiet, feeling worse than I had outside and minutes before. I really had misread the whole situation, and my only defense was that it was Efrem. Anyone else, I would have been able to see clearly, but he was different. He was the only one I couldn't see objectively, I never could. My feelings for him did more than cloud my judgment; they completely obscured everything else around me and particularly, my logic.

"I just wanted to hear about *you*."

"Well, so you know, Thiago Fanton is not a terrorist. He's a gun smuggler and pimp and basically a crime boss, but he has no agenda beyond making money."

"Yeah, I don't care. The other guys in my office can waste their time running that down. I already filed my report that we needed to turn our case over to the FBI because he's not a homegrown terrorist, just another mobster."

"They should take him off the streets."

"I agree, they should. I hope they do, but it has squat to do with Homeland."

"Right."

His gaze traveled over me from head to toe.

"You know, Lee already judged my clothes today," I teased, trying to inject some levity so I could have a moment to get my heart to stop racing, my pulse to stop pounding in my ears, and my stomach to unclench. Ever since I'd seen him, I'd been aroused, my body heating like it hadn't in over a decade. I'd noticed men, how their clothes fit, how their muscles bunched, all the while craving Efrem, wanting Efrem, needing him….

"And thought what?"

"What?" I was really trying to listen but he was right there, standing close to me, smelling good, looking better, and my capacity to parse words was quickly deserting me.

"You said Lee looked you over, what did he think?"

"I don't—what do you think?" I could have killed myself for asking, for fishing, for wanting to hear that he found me as alluring as I found him.

"Well, I think you look great. I love the cardigan and the jeans and the boots and all of it, but mostly I was thinking that I'd like it all off."

I grinned at him, exhaling sharply. "So then, you're not just here for more answers, there might be something else you want too?"

"There's a lot more I want," he husked, lunging at me, taking my face in his hands before he kissed me.

I was six four, and he was three or four inches shorter than me, so we notched together perfectly, easily, like I remembered, my hand on the back of his head, cradling but also keeping him still as I tried to go slow but ended up mauling his mouth.

His kisses were ravenous and hard, bruising my lips as he tried to crawl down my throat, his hands everywhere, clutching my back, digging into my muscles, trying to get me closer.

I shoved him off me and unzipped my cardigan, shrugged it off my shoulders, and let it fall down beside my feet on the floor, joined quickly by my scarf that I hadn't bothered to take off when I lost my jacket earlier.

"Where's your bedroom?" he asked hoarsely, panting as his heated gaze took me in.

I pointed to the archway, and he turned, toeing off his wingtips before heading toward it and the hall beyond.

Following quickly, I admired the long lines of him and the ass I knew would be just as round and firm and beautiful as I remembered.

He sped up, and I was right there behind him, and when he took the right into the enormous master bedroom and wheeled around to face me, I didn't stop, instead scooping him up, throwing him over my shoulder, and carrying him the rest of the way to the California king. I dumped him and then followed, pinning him under me and finding his mouth even as my fingers went to work on his clothes.

He had so many layers still on: sport jacket, vest, dress shirt, and T-shirt. When I growled, he smiled against my mouth and writhed beneath me, pulling my T-shirt out of my waistband and then burrowing underneath and skimming his hands over my skin as he kissed me back just as hungrily as before, his tongue mating with mine, wanting more, taking more, as he bowed up off the bed.

"For fuck's sake," I yelled, rolling off him, settling back on my haunches, glowering at him. "Take all that off!"

He laughed, and the warmth of the sound made me shiver and clench my teeth with the swell of emotions, of things remembered, of how we were in bed, and scared that somehow I'd made it all up or made it more and this time, now, would not live up to his, or my, expectations.

Moving fast, he scrambled over to me, hands on my face, touching me, tracing over my cheeks, my eyebrows, my chin, and my lips. "Tell me. Tell me now," he demanded.

I realized that my hands were shaking. "I—what if it's not... if we're not—" My gaze was on his, holding, not looking away, though everything in me screamed out to run.

He slipped his hand around the back of my head, his fingers pressing on my nape, a place he knew I held tension, always, and just the familiar touch soothed me, let me breathe. When he leaned in for a kiss, I met him halfway; the heat of his mouth reminding me that this was the only man I'd ever loved, and he was here, with me, after forever and wasting time worrying was the epitome of stupid.

"We're good, baby," he promised. "And I want you so badly—look at my hands."

His were shaking as well.

I took his both in mine and smiled at him.

"It's okay, I'm right here, not going anywhere, I swear to God."

"You don't—know."

"I do know."

I shook my head. "I haven't been with—"

"And you think I have?"

My eyes met his, and he held my gaze, unwavering, solid, the blown pupils saying all that he couldn't.

"That's nuts," I croaked out. I was never vulnerable, never at the mercy of someone else, but now just a few words from him had leveled me. "You're telling me that since I was last in your bed, there hasn't been anyone else?"

"How could there be? How could I settle for anyone but you?"

I nodded quickly, the lump in my throat making speech impossible.

"I was in love with you—and I've never stopped loving you."

Gently, slowly, I eased the tweed sport coat off his shoulders, down his arms and off, then I undid the buttons on the vest and removed that as well. It helped me breathe, eased the constriction in my chest, calmed me slowly as I peeled him out of his layers. After I lifted the T-shirt over his head and off, unveiling the sleek golden skin of his chest that had haunted my dreams, I leaned forward and kissed the curve of his shoulder.

"I missed you," he whispered, bucking in my hands as I smoothed them over his ribs, easing him back as I kissed down his throat.

When I reached his chest and the first dark, dusky nipple, I sucked the way I knew he loved, nibbling gently before blowing softly on the taut nub.

"I can't," he whimpered, and I heard how brittle his control was and how close he was to breaking down. "It's been—where is your lube, get it now."

I had some in my nightstand. I'd been celibate, yes, but there were still those nights I thought of him, selected a memory, and stroked myself off.

"Ef—"

"Get it," he pleaded, and the look on his face—dazed, debauched, ready and needy—had me scrambling to do as he asked.

I watched him as he rolled off the bed, tearing at the rest of his clothes and pushing his dress pants down, mesmerized at the sight of him in such a hurry.

He noticed me staring. "What're you *doing*?"

Diving for the nightstand, I yanked out the drawer and spilled everything on the floor, rewarded by the snickering behind me.

"I'm nervous. Shut up," I rumbled, having what I needed, following his example and getting back on my feet, standing beside the bed, shucking out of my clothes as fast as humanly possible, needing everything off, my skin hot, almost feverish.

When I was naked, I looked up, and he was staring at me.

"What?"

He held out his hand, palm up, like he was presenting me.

"Honey?"

"Jesus Christ, Darius, look at you."

I was too busy looking at him. "What do you do, live at the gym?" Underneath his clothes, the man was everything I'd expected, solid, sculpted muscle from the defined six-pack to the carved chest. All of him was chiseled and cut and utterly mouthwatering, and his long, fat dick was hard and leaking and ready for me. His mouth was open as he stared at me, and I had no idea why. "You're beautiful."

"No, I'm all the guys at the club, baby. You, on the other hand.... Christ."

I put a knee on the bed, and he dove toward me, crawling fast, his mouth opening even as his hand closed around my cock.

"You don't—Efrem!"

He took me in like he'd done it yesterday instead of sixteen years ago, making the suction strong as I watched his cheeks hollow out, heard the sexy moan I'd so missed, and felt his fingers slip around my ass as he urged me to fuck his mouth.

I wanted to. I wanted to make him take all of me, but I wanted inside him so desperately that I truly would have killed anyone who stood in my way.

But he tightened his grip, urging me on, faster, faster, and I couldn't think. My body took over, and I pumped between those beautiful plump lips, thrusting into the wet heat, and came with a yell, emptying down the back of this throat. It felt endless, and there was only Efrem swallowing and sucking, then easing back to lick until there was nothing left.

I hadn't realized I'd closed my eyes until they drifted open and I saw him in a sated sprawl under me, his hand covered in cum as aftershocks shuddered through him.

"You came just from sucking my dick?"

He nodded slowly, and I went to my knees beside the bed and kissed his swollen lips, licked into his mouth, and tasted my cum on his tongue. I was hungry for him, to have him under me, crying out and begging, and I ran my fingers through his hair, fisting tight for a moment before letting go, needing to mark him somehow so he'd never leave me again.

"Don't worry," he murmured, heaving for breath, and I realized it was because of me, I wasn't letting him up for air between kisses. "I'm never leaving."

"You have a life. You have a job," I said before I kissed him again, this time sucking on his tongue, rising over him just enough so I could stretch out on top of him. Once I had him under me, I rolled us over so he was on top, draped over me, my hands on his head, keeping him there, locked to me.

He broke the kiss, gasping, and sat up, straddling my hips and reaching for the lube.

I chuckled as I passed him the bottle.

"What's funny?"

"You realize I'm not twenty-nine anymore, right?"

"Meaning?"

"Meaning my recovery time isn't what it used to be."

"How do you know?"

He was right, how did I?

"Well?"

"Yeah, but when I'm taking care of myself," I began, able to have the conversation with Efrem that I couldn't with anyone else, "I never last more than one time."

"Me neither," he admitted, "but I think with you in front of me—I might be inspired."

"Is that right?" I teased.

His grin was wicked. "I think, just maybe, things like age might not apply to us."

And as I wondered if there could be anything to that at all, I felt my body heat once more, the throb of arousal making me shiver.

"There see," he croaked, clearly no less affected than me.

"I waited for you," I told him, watching as he snapped open the lid and dribbled some into his palm.

"I waited for you too," he said, reaching behind him, his fingers feather light on my already thickening cock, slicking me, stroking me, the languid caress causing new flutters of arousal to roll through my body, my mewling cry not a sound I would have credited myself with being able to make.

I gripped his muscled thighs before taking the lube from him, coated my hand and took hold of his beautiful cock, slicking him from balls to head, watching glistening beads of pearly precome slip from the opening.

"Why does your hand feel a thousand times better than mine?"

I chuckled, and it sounded almost sinister, the joy at having him under my power a heady thing. When he lifted, my gaze met his. "You don't have to. I'm in heaven right now."

"I need you," he almost whined, and his hand was on my shaft, moving me forward, into position, and I swallowed my demand for him to hurry.

"It'll be painful this way," I warned, desperate to be inside of him, and just as desperate not to hurt him. "Let me put you on your back."

"I like it this way, you know that," he moaned, and it was long and aching.

"It's been a long time, honey. You need to—"

"I might not have men, but I have toys," he assured me with a wicked grin before his lips parted and his head fell back.

He sank down over me just a fraction, and the sound that came out of him, the hum before the *oh God* and my name, over and over, nearly broke me.

"Go slow," I rasped even as I groaned long and loud, the vise of heat so tight, so hot, opening a fraction at a time, nearly driving me out of my mind.

His head now rolled forward and his eyes locked on mine as he put his right hand down on the middle of my chest, bracing himself as he took me inside.

"I used to want to top," he whispered, sounding dazed, fully seated now, his slippery channel filled with me. "And now I can't for the life of me remember why."

"Because it's fuckin' heaven being buried to my balls in your ass," I rumbled, the contentment of being inside of him almost more than I could bear. Having him stretched around me, his muscles rippling and squeezing, the spasms incessant, pulsing, making me jerk under him like a live wire.

"It's heaven having you inside," he promised, stroking down my abdomen, fingers tracing over the muscles there. "It's like you're at the core of me."

I shivered from the sensations traipsing through my body.

"Shall I move?" he teased, lifting just a bit and slipping back down.

"No, don't do that," I pleaded. "It'll be over too fast."

But he clenched his inner muscles, and I gripped his thighs hard in reaction, wanting it, and not, at the exact same time.

"Let's do that again," he said slyly, but I twisted my body, changed my angle, and he gasped, hands like claws on my chest as I pushed up into him and felt his whole body tremble.

"I think I found the good spot."

"Darius," he whined, and I knew, because I always had, what he needed.

Rolling him to his back, I put the crook of my elbows under his knees and bent him in half, his ass pressed to my groin, and pushed into him as deep as I could go.

He howled my name. I smiled. I'd forgotten he was a yeller.

Pulling out partway, I thrust back inside, my hips pumping, hands curled around his shoulders, using them for leverage as I hammered into him.

His eyes were closed, fists clenched in the blankets, as he cried out for me to not stop, to never stop.

"But you're gonna come in a second, and then we'll do this again and again, all the time, whenever we want because we've been apart fuckin' long enough."

"Don't let me go. Please don't let me go," Efrem begged.

"You don't have to worry. That's never gonna happen again," I promised, setting a pounding, driving rhythm that made it impossible to concentrate on anything but the climax building inside of me. "But you need to come," I said, my voice low, guttural, as I reached between us and began pumping my fist around him to the same steady movement of my cock. "Because I'm too close, and this time is for you."

"Darius!" he roared and arched up under me, his body seized in the throes of a powerful, shuddering release, his muscles clamping down around me triggering mine seconds later.

We sank into a moment of nothing, just a roil of sensation, a wave of aftershocks that shorted out my brain as I collapsed on top of him, taking his mouth and kissing him deeply.

When I could see again, I stared into all that green and breathed.

He put his hands on my face, smiling and crying at the same time.

"I'm gonna pull out in just a second," I lied.

"There's no hurry."

There wasn't. Never again.

CHAPTER NINE

WE LAY there in bed, drinking water and deciding if we were going to cook or venture out into the cold.

"Can you cook now?" he asked.

"I can."

"Oh yeah?" He sighed, rolling sideways, snuggling against my shoulder, his hand over my heart. "What can you cook?"

It was hard to think with his warm skin pressed to mine, his leg draped over my thigh under the covers, and his clean-smelling hair right under my nose. I wanted to kiss him some more, hug him, and have him under me again. I could already tell I was going to have a problem focusing for a bit.

"Hey."

"Sorry," I said softly, pushing his hair back out of his face. "I'm distracted. You're distracting me. How about an omelet?"

"That sounds perfect," he said, shifting to lie on top of me.

"This isn't going to get you food."

"What did you mean when you said 'this time is for you'? Did you think the first time wasn't for me as well?"

"The blow job was for me," I assured him.

"I came just from having your dick in my mouth, so yes, both were for me just as both were for you. When did we ever have sex that the other person didn't enjoy?"

He had a point.

"If we did, I don't remember."

"No, you're right."

"I know I am, so stop thinking that everything needs to be perfect at this exact moment, because it doesn't."

"Okay."

"The important thing is, we're going to stick together, yes?"

I cupped his face in my hands. "That's what I want. Is that what you want?"

His smile was blinding. "Yes."

"Okay," I said, feeling the happiness seep into my bones. "Let me feed you."

I got a kiss in agreement.

LATER, AS he sat on one of the barstools at the island in my kitchen and I stood across from him, leaning over as I ate, I got a small nod.

"Oh, come on, that's a good omelet."

He cackled.

"That's mean."

"Well, that's because I'm mean now."

"Are you?"

"Yes. Ask anyone."

"It could be that since you haven't been laid in sixteen years, you got kind of pissed off and stayed that way."

His low seductive chuckle made my dick hard again.

"Drink your juice," I muttered.

He sighed deeply and then turned on the barstool to look at me. He looked good in my sweats and a long-sleeved Henley. The heavy crew socks I had put on his feet myself, to make sure he stayed warm.

"What's with the look?" I asked, noting how he was studying me.

"I want to tell you everything I've done, everyplace I've been, and then I want you to do the same. I want all the blanks filled in for both of us."

"Me too."

He huffed out a breath. "So I want to sit with tea and talk to you," he said, pointing at the mantle. "Over there by the fireplace."

"Okay, let's do that."

His smile made it feel like there were butterflies now flying around in my chest.

I told him to go sit down, but he didn't listen and did the rest of the dishes for me—there weren't many, I was a clean-as-you-go guy—while I made the tea. I cheated and used the Keurig, but that way it was fast.

He took a seat on my long leather couch, and I followed with the mugs, setting them down before I flipped the switch beside the mantel, and the fire roared to life in front of me. Gas was a wonderful thing, and even though I missed the crackling of the wood, I did not miss cleaning up the ash or the chimney.

"That's nice," he sighed, picking up his mug and taking a sip of tea. As soon as he tasted it, his eyes widened. "You remembered."

"That you like peppermint and Earl Grey together," I said, giving him a half grin. "Why, yes, dear, I did remember."

He patted the seat beside him, and I walked around the other end and followed his direction. Once I was down, I twisted in the seat to face him.

"You ready to hear about my family?"

"Yes." I smiled wide. "But first I have to tell you something."

"What's that?"

"I love you very much."

His shoulders slumped, and he groaned loudly before putting his mug down on the coaster on the table and crawling into my lap.

"How am I supposed to drink my tea?" I complained.

He wrapped his arms around my neck and squeezed tight.

"That's great and all, but really, I wanted some tea."

He nuzzled his face into the side of my neck before he kissed me. "I love you too, you fuckin' idiot."

"Idiot?" I objected. "How so?"

He shoved back, hands on my shoulders, and glared at me. "Why didn't you come find me the second you were done with the military?"

"I couldn't do that. You don't just pop in on the man you love when you're black ops."

"Why not?"

"Well, for one," I said, rubbing his arms, gentling him until he stopped locking his elbows, let them bend, and leaned closer to me. "You're not out at your job."

"I am."

"You are?"

He nodded. "I wasn't five years ago, so I understand what you're saying, but you have to know that I would have done anything to have you back."

It was terrifying. The life I'd had, what I'd done, all the death dealt, all the missions run, the seriously fucked-up shit dependent on absolutely perfect timing requiring nerves made of even stronger stuff than steel, and this man had me shaking like a leaf.

"Baby?" he crooned, hands on the side of my neck, his thumb on the pulse point in my throat. "What's wrong?"

This was why I'd never looked for him, never gone to him, because until I was out, until I was done with working for my government—or anyone else but myself—the distraction of him would have been not only my death, but his as well.

"Once you're in that life, once you're a CIA operative, you don't just ask to be out. They let you go when they're ready or when you become too scary, too unpredictable, with more contacts and resources than even they have, and after you've killed everyone they send after you and return only pieces."

He nodded, taking a quick breath.

"I've only been all the way out, not even a contractor, for a couple years," I explained. "And even then, until the day I told them no and knew nothing was going to happen, I was still worried. But once things were on my terms, I started piecing my life back together."

"And me?"

"I didn't think I could have you and I didn't want to mess up your life."

"Being with you *is* my life, and I can speak from experience," he insisted, hands on my face. "I've had everything but you, and I feel like I've been walking around like a zombie the whole time."

"I didn't have time to do anything but survive for so long," I confessed, "but just in the past six months, things have changed so dramatically for me, and—I want my life back."

"Meaning me."

I nodded, voice lost for a moment, the lump in my throat too big to speak around.

"Right?" he teased, the playfulness there in the crinkle of the laugh lines, the pop of his dimples, and curl of his plump lips. "Your life is me?"

He had always done that, given me the time I needed to recover when there was too much emotion for me to talk through.

"Yes, it is," I assured him.

His eyes filled fast, and I put my hand on his cheek, my thumb brushing away tears. I swallowed hard myself, feeling it, the ground securely under my feet after so many years. We had to bump our foreheads together just as we'd done earlier, gently, the communion necessary, learning things about each other would be the new normal until we got used to each other again, could take for granted that we'd see each other every day. In the meantime, we would be soaking up every brush, touch, kiss, and hug that the other person gave us. It was absolutely necessary. I'd been starving for him for over a decade, if he wanted to stretch out on top of me morning, noon, and night I was more than game.

We sat there, snuggled together in front of the fire, and after what was surely only minutes, I jolted awake, realizing that for once in forever, I'd fallen asleep without a gun within easy reach. I *never* did that, I was always ready. But Efrem was there, warm and heavy in my arms, and I had surrendered to the closeness like I'd had it yesterday instead of years ago.

His effect on me was dangerous, intoxicating, soothing and craved, but if someone came through the front door to hurt us—

"Hey," he murmured before yawning, tightening his hold on me. "What's wrong?"

He couldn't even see my face with his head on my chest, but my breathing alerted him, the way I'd clutched him when I woke up.

"Nothing."

"Liar," he said, chuckling as he sat up so he could meet my gaze. "You worried that I'm going to take away your edge?"

With his drugging kisses, the overwhelming feeling of contentment, and my inability to keep my hands off him, I wouldn't be able to protect either of us if needed. "I'm scared you already have."

"And would that be so bad?"

"I'm worried about you getting hurt."

His smile was warm and sexy at the same time. "You have too many people watching out for you to worry."

"You don't know that."

He snorted. "Oh, I think I do."

And while I sat there counting, I realized he was right. I was safe as houses on that island.

"Tell me something."

"Anything," I agreed, sinking my fingers into his thick hair, feeling so present in my own body as I had not been in years. I was moving slowly, breathing deeply, letting everything but him and me roll away.

"How did you know I'd be waiting?"

"I didn't. I wished, I prayed. I hoped," I admitted, happy to reveal that truth to him.

"Well, I nearly passed out when I saw you in Detroit."

"You," I said like he was nuts. "Holy shit, Ef, what made you pick Homeland?"

"I was recruited."

"And?"

"And it's been harder in some aspects than I thought it would be, easier in others. There's a lot of things, like this one with your friend Trevan, that turn out to not be under our purview, and we end up chasing our tails sometimes, but there are some real wins too."

"So your job is important to you."

"It is, yes."

"That's good. I knew you'd find your niche and be passionate about it."

"I'm passionate about you; the job is of secondary consideration at this point. Like I said, there are a hundred guys that can do it better."

"What, you've been just warming a chair?" I scoffed, reaching out to trace over a golden eyebrow before brushing his hair back, completely unable to stop touching him. "That's not you. If you didn't think you were contributing, you would have stepped aside."

"I'm not saying I'm not good at my job, I'm more than competent," he assured me. "But I'm also ready for the next adventure in my life if they tell me that my administrative leave becomes permanent."

"What will you do then?"

He thought a moment. "I really like it here in Nahant, maybe I'll become a lobsterman."

I couldn't contain my laughter. Just the visual in my head was hysterical.

"I feel that I'm being made fun of."

"No, honey," I said, chuckling, taking his face in my hands and kissing his nose. "Maybe let's give it some more thought."

"Fine."

I kissed him then, long and slow and deep.

"Now." He exhaled sharply, straddling my thighs. "Let me tell you about Calum and the flavor of the month club."

"What?"

"It's what my mother calls the different girls my brother brings to all our holiday gatherings. Last year, the one he brought to Thanksgiving wasn't the same one he brought at Christmas! It's nuts. I have no idea how he's keeping track of them. And he keeps having them get in the pictures, so the photo album is getting kind of dicey, right? My mother is like, what was this one's name?"

I had to laugh along with him because imagining Livia Lahm squinting over her readers and asking her husband, who would be sitting in a chair by the fire, to remember some girl that she didn't want in her holiday album was damn funny. I had been touched when she insisted I get in the very first year Efrem and I were together and for the years after that.

"I can get back in the picture this year right?" I asked him.

"Oh yes," he said before he kissed me breathless.

We were both panting when I broke the kiss.

"I want to hear more about your brother and about your sisters and your folks but first I want to tell you what I do now that can put my military record beyond your reach, and your boss's, and wipe my civilian one like it never existed."

He took a breath before he slipped off my lap and got comfortable beside me, his long legs curled under him.

"I'm the vault," I announced with a little bit of flourish.

He waited, looking at me expectantly.

"Did you hear me?"

"I did."

"Well?" I pressed because everyone I'd told had been amazed or horrified or, in Rahm's case, maybe even a bit put out that it had been me instead of him.

"Well, what?"

"I just told you I was the vault."

"Is that an office or something? Slang for something I should know? Are you the treasurer of some underground—"

"Are you kidding?"

"Don't sound so annoyed. I'm sure whatever it is you do is very important." He placated me like I was a child, smiling indulgently but lovingly at the same time.

"Now you're patronizing me."

"No."

I growled at him, and the answering smile almost made me forget that I was trying to explain something. "Shit, listen to me. The vault is a job."

"Oh?"

"Knock it off. It's a real job and a very important one."

"Who do you work for?"

"You should get comfortable."

Two hours later, because he interrupted me many, many times, he had the idea of what it was I did and had even managed to confuse me a couple of times. It occurred to me as I'd been talking to him that he was very good for me in more ways than one. Beyond Sousanna, and Duncan Stiel, he was the only other person in my life who was not somehow or other, a criminal. Telling him about what I did and having him ask questions was refreshing and reminded me there was more to me than simply what I did.

"What's wrong?" I asked him, concerned with his pained expression.

"I'm terrified of losing you," he said solemnly, lacing his fingers into mine.

"Why would you lose me now?"

"You're traveling all over the world to God knows where, and a lot of those places are dangerous and—"

"You just told me a few hours ago that I should never be afraid here because I have so many people protecting me."

"*Here*, yes," he stressed, scowling, clearly worried. "Not halfway around the world! Who's protecting you *out there*?"

"Did you miss the part where I told you about Ceaton and his team? And you met Lee, so you know he's annoying but terrifying."

He looked scared, worried, and I had to fix that.

"No one wants me dead," I assured him, "except Thiago Fanton."

"And you're not frightened of him at all?"

"Oh, no. There's no one working now who's stupid enough to take a shot at me."

"Yes, but anyone can get off a lucky shot."

"True, but whenever I leave Nahant now, Ceaton's with me, and if you met him and his guys, you'd feel a lot better."

He didn't look convinced.

"I can see if Marko is still next door having tea with my neighbor."

He squinted at me.

"What?"

"That right there does *not* inspire confidence."

I cleared my throat. "You could come with me, if you wanted."

"I'm sorry?"

"I mean, if you're so worried, you could travel with me when I have to go somewhere that could possibly be dangerous."

He climbed back into my lap then, long legs folded on either side of my thighs, hands on my shoulders as he stared into my eyes. "Did I hear you right? You're offering to take a federal agent with you overseas to traffic in stolen goods?"

"Not always stolen, as you heard earlier with Lee. He's going to kill someone so a father can protect his daughter."

"I did hear that, yes."

"So you know it's not always glamorous jet-setting playboy time, and on the other hand, not everyone wants to blow my brains out," I concluded, hands on his hips, shucking him forward, closer to me.

"How often do you travel?"

"So far in the six to seven months, I haven't picked up anything myself," I admitted. "It hasn't been necessary."

He was silent, tracing over my eyebrow with his thumb. "But what if you have to leave tomorrow?"

"Then I will."

"Yes, but—"

"Do you think you'd want to be here when I get back?"

"Be here?"

"You know what I'm asking."

"That's fast," he said, eyes on me, settled on my face,

"It's not."

"Your job and mine," he began hesitantly, "how would that even work?"

"Well, I guess we'll find out," I said. I shrugged. "You're not giving up your job—"

"But I might still be fired."

"Maybe. Maybe not. But either way, I can't give up mine, and I'm not losing you again, so we'll see what we see," I said, sliding my hand around the back of his neck to bring him to me. "You could learn to paint or something."

"I just got you back, and you want me to sabotage our relationship by becoming a kept man?"

"When did I say that? I never said that."

"Darius, you—"

"I don't want to keep you—"

"*What?*"

"No, I mean I don't want to keep you like a sugar daddy or something, I want you to marry me."

He stared at me like he'd seen a ghost, and I sat there waiting.

"That was my line," he husked, hands back on my chest. "I asked you, remember?"

"I do. It's like it happened yesterday, that's how clear it is in my mind."

His breath caught. "And so you want to marry me?"

"Very much."

"I could be a crazy person you know."

"We're both insane. What has that got to do with anything?"

"I—"

"You want to marry me, you always have."

"That's awfully presumptuous of—"

"You have," I insisted, holding on to his thighs when he tried to get up. "Since the first time you met me, you wanted to marry me."

He wasn't arguing.

"You had just come out to your parents, your sisters and brother, your grandmother, everyone, and you were blown away by not only being accepted but by the fact that they all treated it like it was no big deal."

"They all knew already."

"And you were on cloud nine and doing what?"

"I can't believe you remember all this."

I chuckled. "You were happy, and you told me that you were starting your life and not looking for love, but you'd be open to it if it walked in your door."

"Jesus, why did I say all that to you?"

"Because I walked into your office and gave you a raging boner!"

"Conceited much? Holy shit, are you like this with everyone?"

I grabbed his face, holding tight, staring into his eyes. "No. I'm not like this with anyone, ever, except you."

His breath caught as he stared back at me, holding my gaze, unflinching.

"Do you get it? Do you get that I have one shot at being me for the rest of my life if you just fuckin' stay here!"

"I—"

"We can fly out to Washington and pack up your house then go to Connecticut and talk to your parents. I'll explain that there's no prenup, and I'm worth millions now."

He went still. "Is that true?"

I nodded.

"Millions?"

"Yep."

"Are you serious right now?"

"I'm serious about all of it. The marriage proposal, what I'm worth, what—"

"I don't give a shit about money, you know that."

"I do know that, mister old money."

"You—"

I growled. "Just fuckin' marry me!"

"Oh, that's romantic."

"Have we not been separated for sixteen years? Do we not deserve to be together now?"

He scowled at me, and that was surprising. "Oh, I'm not ever leaving," he said flatly. "I'm never leaving. I'm moving in next week. I'll put my place on the market, like, tomorrow."

"I—what?"

He gave me a slow grin that made his eyes sparkle and shine. "And yes, Mr. Hawthorne, I will marry you, and you will come to Essex with me and talk to my parents because they both fell in love with you too."

He had a great family, and I couldn't wait to reconnect with them after all these years. "Yes, well, I'm hard not to love."

"It's true."

I took a breath, feeling my life starting to finally fall into place.

"Tell me something."

"Anything."

"Why didn't you ever sleep with anyone else?"

"I told you already. I was holding out for you."

"But why?"

"Because I love you."

"But that's also the reason you stayed away," he whispered, his voice bottoming out fast.

"Yes."

"Because I would have been in danger too."

"You would have."

"But you thought, any day I can go back, and he'll want me."

I nodded. "As I said before, I held on to that hope."

"And along with that you thought, I better not fuck anyone else or Efrem'll kill me."

I smiled just a little because no, I wasn't ever scared, it was that there was only one Efrem, and he was it for me. It was him or nothing, and so I'd gone without. But I had him now, and there was no getting away. He was mine, I was his, simple as that. It was ridiculous for us to ever be alone again.

"And mostly it was okay because you were busy, and people were trying to kill you, and your job was to kill them, and things were insane, but sometimes—"

"All the time," I corrected. "I missed you all the time."

He curled forward and kissed me, and my lips parted, just as they had the first time all those years ago behind the pool hall. Months later, I'd walked into his house behind him when we got back from training, and he'd kissed me, right after he explained he was being transferred to another unit.

We were basically living together even though we had to maintain separate residences, spending all our free time together, and I was confused and hurt as to why he wanted to leave me.

"Not you," he said, chuckling, smiling as the flush stole up his throat, blotching in large patches and pinking his cheeks. It was so appealing and only I ever caused the reaction. "I never want to leave you."

"Then why?" I asked sharply, not caring if the neighbors heard us or saw us, taking hold of his hips and stepping into his space, inhaling his scent as I licked my lips, wanting to taste him again even as I was angry and even hurt. "Why are you leaving when everything's going so great?"

"I'm not leaving the base," he soothed me, hands on my face. "Just your unit."

"I don't get it."

"It's because I want to kiss you," he answered quickly, arms coiling around my neck as he pressed against me, shivering with the closeness. "I want us to be in two different units so we can take time off at the same time and no one will think twice about it, and I want all that more than I want to give you orders."

I smirked. "You don't wanna give me orders?"

He caught his breath. "I do, but I don't want there to be any power imbalance between us. I want you to want to do what I ask, not to have to, not to ever think in the back of your mind that I could, or would, hurt you."

And I never had until the mistake we both made at the same time in the interrogation room.

"It's just like that day in my house when I told you I was leaving the unit," Efrem said in the present. "We're making a change so we can go forward, together."

Yes, we were.

"Whatever happens from here on out, I want us to do it together."

"It's time," I told him, wrapping my arms around him as he leaned into me.

"For what?"

"For our happily ever after."

"Yes, it is," he agreed, nestling in against me, melting into my arms, surrendering up his weight as he draped himself over me. "It most certainly is."

AUTHOR'S NOTE

MEET CONRAD for the first time in *Mine*.

Read Trevan and Landry's love story in *Mine*.

Meet Ceaton, Pravi, Marko, and the rest of the team in *A Day Makes*.

Get the story of Rahm's meeting with the US marshal in *All Kinds of Tied Down*.

Follow the gun! Read *Acrobat* and *Tied Up in Knots*.

MARY CALMES believes in romance, happily ever afters, and the faith it takes for her characters to get there. She bleeds coffee, thinks chocolate should be its own food group, and currently lives in Kentucky with a five-pound furry ninja that protects her from baby birds, spiders, and the neighbor's dogs. To stay up to date on her ponderings and pandemonium (as well as the adventures of the ninja), follow her on Twitter @MaryCalmes, connect with her on Facebook, and subscribe to her Mary's Mob newsletter.

A DAY MAKES

Mary Calmes

First From The Vault

Mob enforcer Ceaton Mercer has killed a lot of people in a lot of different ways—he stashed the last two bodies in a toolshed belonging to a sweetheart marine researcher in an idyllic island community—but he's really not such a bad guy. Over time he's found a home of sorts, and he even learns he's found a place in the hearts of the people he works with… at least enough so that they won't put a bullet in his head because he's outlived his usefulness to the boss.

But he never thought he'd find one day could change his life, and he's about to discover how wrong he is.

Because in a single day, he meets the man who looks to be *the* one, the love of his life. It's an improbable idea—a man who deals in death finding love—but it's like it's meant to be. That single day gets weirder and troubles pile up, forcing Ceaton to take a hard look at his dreary life and accept that one day *can* change everything, especially himself. His future might be brighter than he expects—if he can stay alive long enough to find out.

www.dreamspinnerpress.com

Mary Calmes

MANGROVE
Stories

Come to beautiful Mangrove, Florida, a tropical paradise where the days are hot, the nights are sultry, and love is in the air, carried by a blue ocean breeze. Don't miss these heartwarming romances by Mary Calmes.

In *Blue Days*, Dwyer Knolls and Takeo Hiroyuki defy tradition and risk their careers for a chance at romance—and the hope that their connection is worth everything they'll sacrifice.

Kelly Seaton and Cosimo Renaldi have been through war, injury, and starting over together. Are they ready to face their pasts and become more than friends in *Quiet Nights*?

Best friends Hutch Crowley and Mike Rojas would make a perfect couple—and everyone sees it but them! Maybe the rest of the town can help them find what they've been missing in *Sultry Sunset*.

Will rent boy Lazlo Maguire get a second chance with the only man he never viewed as a transaction, Britton Lassiter? Or will the secrets that tore them apart before ruin their future in *Easy Evenings*?

Can Fire Chief Essien Dodd's daughter help him and Roark Hammond get together and escape their loneliness in *Sleeping 'til Sunrise*? With strong emotions and past hurts at play, focusing on what's most important won't be easy.

www.dreamspinnerpress.com

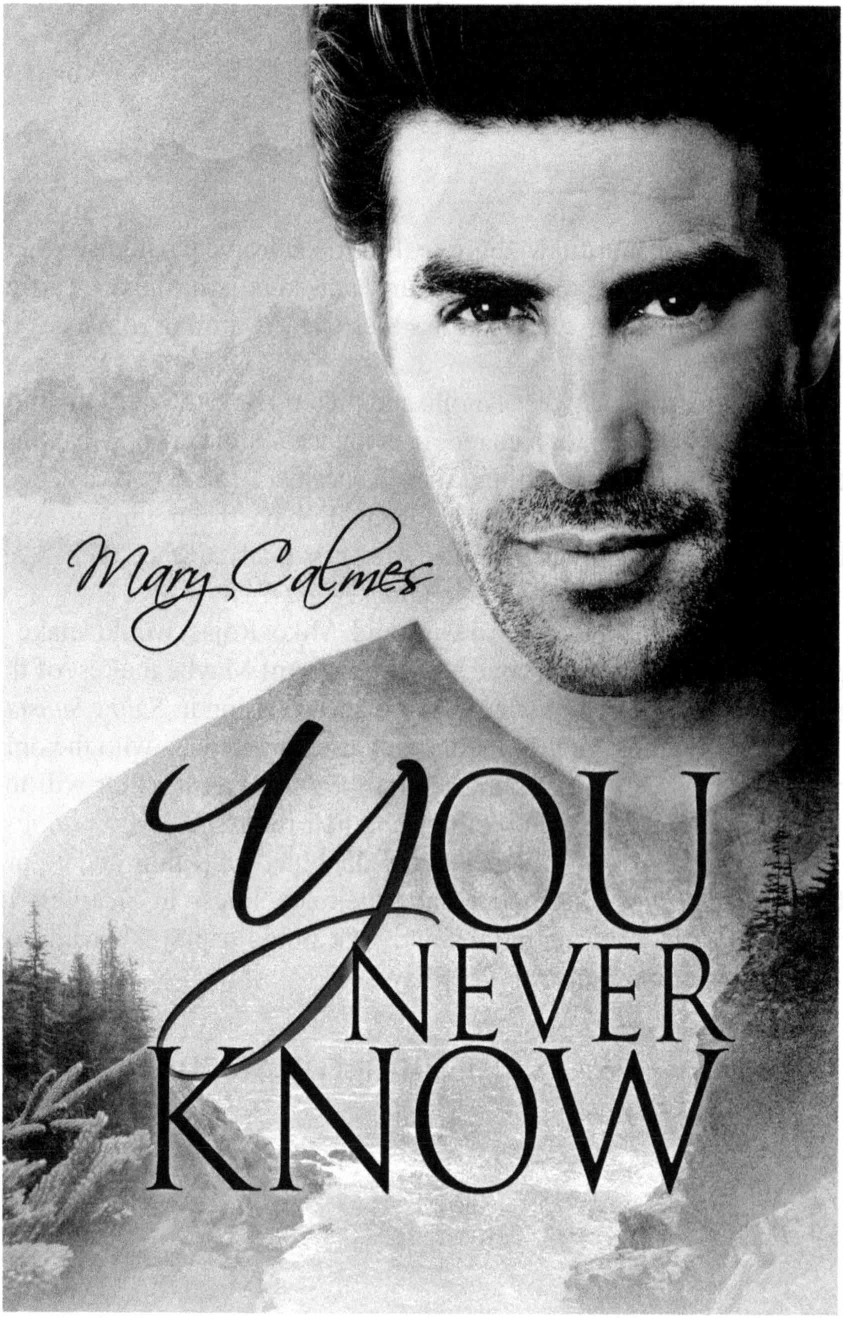
Mary Calmes
YOU NEVER KNOW

Hagen Wylie has it all figured out. He's going to live in his hometown, be everybody's friend, explore new relationships, and rebuild his life after the horrors of war. No muss, no fuss is the plan. He's well on his way—until he finds out his first love has come home too. Hagen says it's no big deal, but a chance encounter with Mitch Thayer's two cute sons puts him directly in the path of the only guy he's never gotten out of his head.

Mitch returned for three reasons: to raise his sons where he grew up, to move his furniture business and encourage it to thrive, and to win Hagen back. Years away made it perfectly clear the young man he loved in high school is the only one for him. The problem? He left town and they have not talked since.

If Hagen's going to trust him again, Mitch needs to show him how he's grown up and isn't going to let go. They could have a new chance at love… but Hagen is insistent he's not reviving a relationship with Mitch. Then again, you never know.

www.dreamspinnerpress.com

TIMING

Mary Calmes

Timing: Book One

Stefan Joss just can't win. Not only does he have to go to Texas in the middle of summer to be the man of honor in his best friend Charlotte's wedding, but he's expected to negotiate a million-dollar business deal at the same time. Worst of all, he's thrown for a loop when he arrives to see the one man Charlotte promised wouldn't be there: her brother, Rand Holloway.

Stefan and Rand have been mortal enemies since the day they met, so Stefan is shocked when a temporary cease-fire sees the usual hostility replaced by instant chemistry. Though leery of the unexpected feelings, Stefan is swayed by a sincere revelation from Rand, and he decides to give Rand a chance.

But their budding romance is threatened when Stefan's business deal goes wrong: the owner of the last ranch he needs to secure for the company is murdered. Stefan's in for the surprise of his life as he finds himself in danger as well.

www.dreamspinnerpress.com

AFTER THE
SUNSET

Mary Calmes

Timing: Book Two

Two years after riding off into the sunset with ranch owner Rand Holloway, Stefan Joss has made a tentative peace with his new life, teaching at a community college. But the course of true love never does run smooth. Rand wants him home on the ranch; Stef wants an exit strategy in case Rand ever decides to throw him out. Finally, after recognizing how unfair he's being, Stef makes a commitment, and Rand is over the moon.

When Stef gets the chance to prove his devotion, he doesn't hesitate—despite the risk to his health—and Rand takes the opportunity to show everyone that sometimes life's best surprises come after the sunset.

www.dreamspinnerpress.com

WHEN THE DUST SETTLES

Mary Calmes

A Timing Story

Glenn Holloway's predictable life ended the day he confessed his homosexuality to his family. As if that wasn't enough, he then poured salt in the wound by walking away from the ranch he'd grown up on, to open the restaurant he'd always dreamed of. Without support from his father and brother, and too proud to accept assistance from anyone else, he had to start from scratch. Over time things worked out: Glenn successfully built a strong business, created a new home, and forged a life he could be proud of.

Despite his success, his estrangement from the Holloways is still a sore spot he can't quite heal, and a called-in favor becomes Glenn's worst nightmare. Caught in a promise, Glenn returns to his roots to deal with Rand Holloway and comes face-to-face with Mac Gentry, a man far too appealing for Glenn's own good. It could all lead to disaster—disaster for his tenuous reconnection with his family and for the desire he didn't know he held in his heart.

www.dreamspinnerpress.com